The Skies Above

A Story of Hope

ARZOO FAIZ

Arzoo Faiz—The skies above: a story of hope
ISBN: 978-1-7642731-0-7 (paperback)

A catalogue record for this book is available from the National Library of Australia

Front cover illustration: Nazaneen Faiz
Editing: Kristina Proft
Delphian Books
+61 2 8625 5530

Printed in Australia

Please see the Glossary on page 271 for words in the Dari language of Afghanistan.

I dedicate this book to my amazing daughter Nazy, wonderful son Noah, my parents for always having my back, my beautiful extended family, my best friend my husband and last but not least, to the amazing women of Afghanistan; resilient and courageous!

Chapter 1

My cheeks were red and throbbing with pain from Mother's unexpected slap.

"You spoiled greedy girl!" Mother said in a sharp tone.

I was not sure what I had done to make her so angry. I had only said "Yes please," when she asked if I'd like some watermelon.

"You have just arrived home from Samira's birthday party, and you already want to eat again!" she said resentfully.

Samira's birthday party had been lots of fun, with games and activities at every corner. I'd been entrenched in the festivities of the day and even though there was an abundance of food on offer, my focus had been on making the most of my time with my friends. Mother was right—there had been a lot of food at the party—the buffet was full of delicious food and decadence. However, she didn't know that I had turned down Samira's mother's numerous offers throughout the day for me to eat something.

The tears rolled down my cheeks without effort. I was confused, I didn't know it was a trick question. I ran into the bedroom I shared with my older brother Imran and threw myself onto my bed, sobbing uncontrollably.

I felt so hurt. I loved eating watermelon. Why would she hit me for no real reason? *Does she even love me? I wondered.*

Mother didn't get angry with Imran as quickly as she did with me. I always seemed to upset her, even when I tried so hard not to.

Sometimes I think it's because I'm nothing like her—not in personality, not even in looks. Imran has her deep brown eyes, her pale skin, her easy charm. He made people laugh without even trying. Maybe she saw more of herself in him than in me.

Here in Pakistan, the days dragged by, heavy with heat and endless talk about leaving. Everyone spoke of migrating overseas, chasing a brighter future. Bahba would smile and talk about "a land where opportunity thrives, and dreams come true." I'd hear him whisper to Mother late at night about it, as if planning the way to heaven—the same heaven *Mullah* talked about in scripture class.

I heard the doorbell ring. I raised my head

slightly from my tear-dampened pillow to the sound of Mother's voice. "Who is it?"

"It's me, Injilla," replied a gently spoken voice.

I jumped out of bed with excitement, wiping my face. From my bedroom I could hear Grandmother, Uncle Bilal and Aunt Inji greeting Mother as they came into the house.

My tears disappeared and were replaced by a cheerful smile as I jumped out of bed and made my way into the living room.

I was so happy to hear Aunt Inji's voice. She was Mother's younger sister.

I stared at her briefly as she stood there in our living room, looking the epitome of kindness and grace.

"*Salam jhan,*" she said as she stepped forward and greeted me, hugging me and giving me a peck on the cheek.

"*Salam* Aunt Inji," I replied with a big grin on my face. I was the only one who called her Aunty "Inji," my special name for her.

"I am going to miss you so much my little one," she said with tears filling up in her eyes.

"Are you all packed and ready for your flight tomorrow?" Mother rudely interjected.

The realisation hit me like a ton of bricks. Aunty

Inji, Uncle Bilal and Grandmother were all going to a wonderful place called Australia. They had been desperately praying to go there for as long as I could remember.

I wished I could go with Aunt Inji to that wonderful country where we could be safe and happy and never think about war again.

"I packed my bag, Mother's bag and Bilal's bag," Aunt Inji said, slightly annoyed that our moment together had been interrupted.

My Grandfather had passed away when Aunt Inji was only six years old, so she'd had to grow up fast and take over the role of head of the family. She took care of Grandmother and her younger brother Bilal, even though she was only seventeen. But she was still a child at heart, making up for the childhood she missed out on while taking care of the family.

Uncle Bilal was younger than Aunt Inji by two years. He was tall with hazel-coloured eyes and dusty brown hair. Always in a good mood, he was lots of fun to be around, playing games with me and Imran and creating the distraction that we all desperately needed in our difficult circumstances.

When they left for Australia, I would especially miss Grandmother's soothing voice telling me stories about the old days in Kabul before the Russians invaded our beautiful Motherland.

I loved it when she spoke longingly about the fresh air of Paghman and the taste of the sweet juicy fruits of Kabul, the welcoming and hospitable nature of the people, their strength and resilience.

I wanted to experience the beauty and enchantment that Grandmother spoke of in her stories about her childhood in Afghanistan, where clear blue skies were filled with flocks of birds gliding in the fresh air, soaring so high without a care in the world.

I hoped that one day, when I was older, I could go to Afghanistan and see the beauty and enchantment for myself. I prayed that the natural landscapes would not perish with time at the hands of the brutal war that was raging. I wished that, when the war was over and the guns were gone, the smell of gunpowder would vanish, leaving crisp, fresh mountain air.

I longed to go there and taste those fruits and breathe in the mountain air and be around people who understood my language and I in turn would understand theirs.

These memories that Grandmother shared were everything to me; a connection linking me to my family's heritage. I was born in "beautiful Afghanistan," as Grandmother so fondly referred to it, and came to Pakistan when I was just a baby. My family had not been back since the war began.

Grandmother's gentle voice took me back to the days when everyone in my family was happy, when life was free from the fear, grief, loss, and pain that war brings. I gave Grandmother a heartfelt hug as I welcomed her into the house.

Of course I would miss Aunt Inji the most. I would be longing for her warm, gentle cuddles.

I always wondered why Mother was nothing like her sister. Mother was not very affectionate, nor did she give hugs. Come to think of it, there was no resemblance between Aunt Inji and Mother in any way. Aunt Inji had thick black curly hair like a dark crepe veil and mysterious hazel eyes that matched her olive complexion. She was tall and slender with a beautiful pair of dimples that complement her smile.

Mother, though also tall, was curvaceous and had straight, sleek, long brown hair like silk. She had beautiful, curious big brown eyes and a peculiar kind of laugh when she was over-excited.

Aunt Inji and Mother were born several years apart but they had a close bond despite their opposite natures. Mother enjoyed cooking, shopping, and decorating the house with the latest home furnishings, whereas Aunt Inji wrote poetry, loved to read and tell stories and was very passionate about education. More specifically, educating girls, because as Aunt Inji often said, "If you educate a girl, they grow up to have the knowledge to educate the whole family." I looked at them in awe and wished I too had a sister who I could share all my secrets with. It would be like having a best friend who was also related to you; someone who you were forever connected with, in a lifelong bond.

"Say goodbye to Aunt Injilla now because you and Imran are not going to the airport tomorrow. It's too early for you two to get up and get ready. Your Uncle Anwar will come late tonight to stay with you and your brother," Mother said, as she signalled me and Imran with a movement of her head to go to bed.

I didn't want to say goodbye to Aunt Inji, not now, not ever. The possibility of not seeing her again tore me up inside. I couldn't imagine life without her and secretly wished that she was my mother, that I was her princess for real. Of course, that wasn't possible, so I just wished she could take me with her. Mother said that we'd be on our way to

Australia soon too, but we didn't know when. This just wasn't good enough for me. What if I never saw her again?

"One thing is for sure, that I will miss you the most princess," Aunt Inji said tearfully as she cupped my face in the palms of her hands before pulling me into her arms. Tears rolled down my cheeks as I clung to Aunt Inji, not knowing when I would be able to hold her so close again.

"Princess, think of this time apart as a good thing, in that by the time you all join us in Australia, I will have banked up many new stories to share with you," she said in a caring and convincing tone.

I managed to work up a smile to let her know I approved. After saying goodbye to Uncle Bilal, Grandmother, and Aunty Inji, I slowly made my way towards my bedroom. The thought of Uncle Anwar looking after us made me feel even worse.

Uncle Anwar was Dad's younger brother. Whenever he came over Imran and I always seemed to be running around after him, like making cups of tea or bringing his shoes from the rack. I never thought he really liked children or even understood them. He never wanted to play Snakes and Ladders with us or read to us at night.

Mother always said that family was everything,

so I had no choice but to be polite and respectful to him. "We must respect all the adults in the family, no matter what!" she would insist.

* * *

Later that night, I woke up abruptly in bed feeling sweaty and hot like I had something heavy on top of me. As my eyes adjusted to the darkness, I was able to make out Uncle Anwar's face as he got off me and moved slowly away from my bed and towards the door. *What was he doing in my bed?* My breathing was laboured after the weight on me, and I felt uncomfortable and confused.

Mother had prepared a special guest bedroom for visitors or family if they wanted to sleep over. On occasions Aunt Inji, Uncle Bilal, Grandmother and Uncle Anwar had all stayed in the guest bedroom at some point. This didn't feel right. I lay motionless in my sweaty pyjamas, feeling upset by the night's events.

After some hours, to my relief, I could hear Mother's voice in the hallway. Dawn was breaking.

Suddenly the realisation that Aunt Inji had gone to Australia hit me again. I felt a sunken heavy feeling in the pit of my stomach and my heart was bereft knowing that I was apart from the two people who I loved so dearly, and God knows for how long.

Chapter 2

I stared out the window at a corn seller on the street, pushing his cart. "Warm juicy corn, come get your warm juicy corn!" he called as he trundled down the road.

I would usually alert Mother at the arrival of the corn seller to buy Imran and me juicy corn cobs topped with freshly squeezed lemon juice and chili flakes. The thought of corn would usually cause me to salivate but today it reminded me of Aunt Inji, as she too likes corn. It made me feel more miserable.

Everything in the house reminded me of Grandmother, Aunt Inji and Uncle Bilal, making me even more aware of their absence. My heart felt heavy with loneliness. It was like a piece of it had been snatched right out of my chest and nothing could ever matter to me again.

My tears had dried up now and only the pain remained. It had only been two months since they had gone but every hour that passed felt like a year.

I missed Aunt Inji more than I could use any

words to describe. I missed her like the ocean misses the shoreline as it comes back repeatedly in the form of a wave, to eagerly hug the sand repeatedly. I pined to see her beautiful face, to hear her soft and gentle voice and feel her tender hugs again.

I lay the *sofra* down on the rug in preparation for dinner, making sure it lay nice and flat on the floor, then stood next to Mother in the kitchen. She was like a machine switched on to auto pilot going about her routine like nothing was wrong. Her eyes were swollen from the tears she had shed in secret at night in bed or while Imran and I were at school and Bahba was at work. I could see the sadness in her eyes, longing for her family.

Grandmother would say, "A person's eyes are a window to their heart." I could see that Mother's heart was grieving now.

I wished Mother would let me in and allow me into her heart. I might have been young, but I had a 'high level of emotional intelligence', according to Grandmother. If she could have shared her sadness with me, we could have helped each other heal, rather than suffering in silence.

"Here, take this and place it in on the *sofra*," Mother said as she handed me a tray of rice with meat balls.

I took the large tray and placed it down as she had asked. Soon, Bahba and Imran joined us and we were all seated on the floor around the small *sofra* in preparation to have dinner.

Every night since their departure, the mood had been the same around the *sofra*. It's like the moon would mourn throughout the day, in pure anticipation of seeing the stars once again when darkness falls. We were all feeling the hurt and sadness that separation brings over people.

We all stared at the food without a word for several minutes. Tonight, Mother burst into tears. There wasn't a dry eye around the *sofra*.

I felt so sorry for Mother. The separation had made Mother soft and tender. Her usual façade of perfection could not hide her deeply felt emotions. I wanted to comfort her but didn't know how to. We all wept that night in union, encased in the sorrow that the distance from our beloved ones had caused.

I especially felt Grandmother's absence at after dinner time when the *sofra* was cleared, and all the dishes had been washed. That was when she would sit on the *toshak* that lay on the floor in the living room, leaning back comfortably on her cylinder-shaped under-arm cushion. She would fondly recall memories of her childhood, growing up in the busy capital city of Kabul. It was the time when Grandmother lived with all her cousins, uncles, and aunts in one big house; each family had their own room in the house, but the rest of the amenities were shared by all the families.

They didn't have the material things that Imran and I enjoyed, so I have been told, but instead they had the luxury of peace and being surrounded by the love of family. She called it "those good old golden days," when they were free from the stress of war. It was a time when children could play happily and safely on the streets of Kabul while the mothers dawdled near the well, chatting and drawing water for the day's cooking and washing.

Grandmother reminisced about playing in the backyard, hiding under the blooming grape vines and running around the boysenberry trees—picking handfuls of the sweet juicy fruit as they brushed past them. All the children in the house would play together, making memories and forming lifelong friendships. The families played, studied, and ate together and sometimes had quarrels too.

Grandmother told us tales of the beauty of Kabul that revealed itself in the skies every night and the fresh cool air that made its way through the tall, majestic mountains.

How I missed Grandmother's sweet gentle voice and her animated stories that fuelled my passion and love for a country that I had never seen or experienced with my own eyes. She had kept my love and passion for my Motherland alive in my heart in the hope that one day I too could experience the beauties and secrets of the enchanting Afghanistan.

Chapter 3

"Don't look so worried. I have asked Uncle Anwar to come by later to help you with your mathematics homework," Mother said. "I know maths isn't your favourite subject and you need that extra support," she added cheekily.

I struggled to return the smile. My mind wandered back to the night when Mother and Bahba had gone to the airport to farewell Aunt Inji, Uncle Bilal and Grandmother. I still couldn't make sense of why Uncle Anwar was in my bed on top of me or why he was even in my bedroom at all. I had rerun that night through my head so many times that I even wondered if it had been a figment of my imagination or an awful nightmare that I had abruptly awoken from. Somehow it felt better to think that it wasn't even real and had never happened.

The doorbell rang and brought me back to the present.

"Salaams," Uncle Anwar said to Mother as she

opened the door to let him in.

"*Walekum asalam.* Too busy to visit us now days?" Mother said with a sarcastic laugh.

"I have been meaning to come by, but I'm just so busy with work and all," he replied as he took off his shoes and entered the house. He came towards me and kissed me on the cheek to greet me.

I had casually obliged by offering my cheek even though my mind was consumed by circulating thoughts and confusion.

"That's okay I understand, I'm only teasing. Thank you so much for looking after Zahra. I'll just be at the doctor's and I promise I won't be too long—half an hour max," Mother said as she rummaged around to gather her handbag and keys.

"There are lots of leftovers in the fridge so help yourself and please don't forget to help Zahra with her maths homework. I would have asked Imran but he's gone with his Bahba to the markets. See you later," Mother said happily as she headed toward the door.

It was good to see Mother smile again after so long. She had been very down lately, feeling isolated and lonely due to the absence of her family.

"Zahra, please be good to Uncle Anwar and listen to him," Mother smiled sweetly, closing the door behind her.

Once Mother left, I slowly made my way towards my study nook in my bedroom and sat down in preparation to do my homework. I could hear Uncle Anwar's footsteps not far behind me.

"Mathematics can be fun and exciting for you now at your age. It all depends on how it's taught," Uncle Anwar said with a weird smile on his face.

I looked up at him from my study nook and nodded my head as if to show that I understood what he meant.

"Let me demonstrate." He signalled me to stand up in front of him with his hand. I made my way towards him and stood still in front of him. Suddenly, I felt uncomfortable being alone with Uncle Anwar. I had never felt this way about him before, but it must be something to do with those unexplained events in my bed that night.

Uncle Anwar was a tall man with deep brown hair and was chubby with a round tummy. Bahba would often say how much his brother loved food. They are not remarkably close, but I know Bahba is immensely proud of his little brother. Uncle Anwar works in a big company as an engineer. "If you put Anwar in front of any sort of broken machine, he will fix it in a flash," Bahba would say.

"Good girl. Now turn your back towards me," Uncle Anwar said in a calm and composed tone.

While I had my back towards him, he wrapped his left arm around the middle section of my body. I felt his fat stomach pressing against my back. With his right hand he lifted the back of my white summer dress that Grandmother had made for my birthday party last year.

He pulled at my underwear and placed his hand inside, grabbing hold of the front part of my privates. My entire body became frozen in fear, like I had turned into a statute. While in that position, he then raised me up off the floor and placed his head close behind my right ear and spoke to me in a soft voice.

"Now you are to count all the books on the bookshelf, out loud, one by one," he said, nodding towards the bookcase next to the study nook that Bahba had built for me.

I was numb with fear and could not get any words to come out of my mouth.

"I said count," Uncle Anwar said for a second time, but this time in a commanding tone, while keeping his voice steely, yet soft.

I had counted the books on the bookshelf several times over, but he still insisted that I continue counting. I wondered if this was to help me learn to count, but I have counted the books several times now and he knows that I can count to 100.

What was happening? Why was he doing this? I knew that this was not how they taught maths at school. Neither has Mother or Bahba ever taught me to count like this. Bahba would say, "Use your fingers to help you count and even your toes if you need to."

I was physically in the room, but it was like I was out of my body and felt myself freeze up even more and shut down, almost like the rag doll Mother made me two years ago—all floppy head, arms, and legs. I wanted to scream and cry out, but I couldn't. And if I could have, who could I have screamed to?

I was in turmoil, trying to focus on counting but also trying to make sense of what was happening. My stomach was turning, and I knew from the feeling inside me that what was happening was not right.

But Uncle Anwar was Bahba's brother and his only surviving family member in the world. Mother and Bahba always said that "blood is thicker than water" and that I had to respect my elders. I thought that meant that I should respect the elders in the family, listen to them and be kind to them. So Uncle

Anwar wouldn't intentionally do anything to harm me in any way, right?

Just then Mother's high-heeled shoes tapped out her arrival on the entrance outside the front door. As I heard Mother jiggling the keys to unlock the front door, Uncle Anwar quickly placed me back on the floor, adjusted my underwear and in a nervous voice asked me whether I wanted a cup of tea as he headed towards the kitchen. I don't know why he asked me this as I had never drunk tea in my life!

"See I told you it won't take long!" I heard Mother say.

I burst into tears and tried to run past Mother, but she stopped me and raised my chin to look at me in the face. "Hey, what's the matter Zahra?" in a slightly concerned tone.

I managed to pull away from Mother and headed straight into the bathroom, closed the door behind me and sat on the floor crying. I was sore and stinging and in pain down there.

I could hear Mother playfully ask, "What happened Anwar? I hope you were not too hard on her with the maths work?"

I heard Uncle Anwar's nervous chuckle as he made his way towards the hallway.

"Children are not your strong suit, that's for sure.

Thanks for today." Mother said goodbye to Uncle Anwar, and I heard the door close shut.

That night I gazed out the window at the stars thinking about what had unfolded earlier that day with Uncle Anwar. I felt so angry and confused, but I was not sure why. Mother said that he was there to help me with my maths work and look after me and keep me safe. He would not intentionally hurt me, would he?

Chapter 4

The warmth of the sun brushed my face as I looked up at the sky.

"Come on! Keep up Zahra!" Imran shouted as he ran to fetch the ball.

There's nothing more fun than a good game of cricket. After all, Bahba says this is Pakistan's national sport which they adore and admire. They feel at one with the game "like the blood that runs through their veins!" Bahba says.

I liked playing cricket with Imran but watching it on TV was rather boring as it dragged on for hours. And I had no idea why the referee blew the whistle when the players did the wrong thing. But Bahba and Imran loved it and would be glued to the TV together, shouting and carrying on, whether or not their favourite team won or lost.

But at least playing with Imran carried my thoughts away from what had happened with Uncle Anwar. I felt haunted and scared that he would hurt me again.

Should I tell Mother or Bahba? Maybe they already know? Is it okay for him to do this?

My mind feels like a Ferris wheel just spinning with such thoughts and emotions. Will I get into trouble with Mother for this and get a beating? I didn't know what to think and I felt so alone.

"Don't worry Imran, I'm ready when you are," I said as I raised the cricket bat.

I wanted to talk to Imran about Uncle Anwar to see if he was also doing the same thing to him as me—maybe he was also being hurt in the same way as I had been. *Dear God, I pray that he hasn't. If I tell him and he goes and tells Mother, then I will get into deep trouble.*

Imran is a kind and good big brother. He can be bossy sometimes, stubborn and doesn't always share, but apart from that, he is a great big brother. He was always watching over me and protecting me. Like whenever I had a bad dream, he let me sleep on the corner of his bed and reassured me that there were no such things as monsters or ghosts living inside our big brown wardrobe.

As we walked back home from the park I looked up at Imran, walking next to me swinging the cricket bat casually. *Thank you, God, for giving me such a wonderful brother.*

"What are you looking at stinky? You seem like you are miles away. Come on, I'll race you home," he said as he started running towards our unit.

We both entered the door puffed out and gasping for air.

"Just the two people I wanted to talk to," Bahba said with a grin on his face as he closed the front door behind us.

"I have some wonderful news to share with you both. You will love it, I'm sure! Go quickly and wash up and we shall speak about it over dinner," Bahba said excitedly.

Wonder and excitement filled our faces as we ran towards the bathroom. *What can the good news be?* I wondered.

After washing my hands, I sat opposite Mother on the *sofra* that lay on the floor and Imran sat opposite Bahba, the same places where we sat every night.

"What is the news Bahba? Have we won the lottery?" Imran asked, laughing excitedly.

"No son, unfortunately we haven't won the lottery, but this is the next best thing I suppose," Bahba said as he tore a bite size piece of Afghan naan bread and dipped it in Mother's homemade mint yogurt dip.

"We will soon be heading to Australia to join your grandmother, Aunt Injilla and Uncle Bilal! The pain of waiting and wondering is finally over!" Bahba's face broke into a smile as he looked across to Mother.

I was elated in my mind, but my body just stood still, while Imran managed to get up and run around us, cheering with excitement.

"Woo-hoo, woo-hoo!" Imran screamed, spinning a hand towel in the air in celebration.

I conjured up enough strength to get up and dive into Bahba's arms.

Bahba embraced me tightly. I could smell the spicy aftershave on him that Mother had bought for him on his birthday. There was not a lot of hugging and kissing in my family. Affection was a rarity that was left for special occasions such as birthdays or Eid or when greeting a guest with three kisses on the cheeks. I don't think I can ever recall Mother or Bahba giving me a peck on the cheek or a warm cuddle out of the blue, purely out of love.

"I thought you would be jumping for joy, with the thought of seeing your Aunt Injilla again who you miss so much. I have noticed you have not been yourself since she left to go to Australia," Bahba said as he drew his head back to look at my face covered in tears.

Bahba was right. I was very happy that I was going to see Aunt Inji but ever since the thing that happened with Uncle Anwar while he was helping me with my maths homework, I have been feeling empty and anything that used to bring me joy has evaporated since that day.

Since then, I have so often wondered whether I should tell someone. And if I should, who should I tell? And what if they didn't believe me? What if it gave Mother another reason to like me the least out of me and Imran?

Moving to Australia might just be the thing I need to get away from this nightmare, I thought.

Then suddenly the realisation hit me. *Would Uncle Anwar be coming with us or would he stay here?* I prayed that he would stay or go somewhere far away from me so that he could never do what he did to me again!

For the first time in a long time, I was seeing my family happy, laughing with excitement as we chatted around the *sofra* while we ate dinner. Mother was crying again tonight, but this time, they were happy tears of excitement from the joy of being reunited with her family once again.

I wanted to believe there was a future waiting

for us, something good that God had planned for my family. But thinking about it made me ache too, because maybe there was no hope for the "beautiful Afghanistan," the way Grandmother always described it. I kept wondering if things would ever change, if I'd ever set foot in that land I'd only heard about in stories.

The next day Uncle Anwar came for dinner to share and celebrate the good news.

I was ruminating about the other day's maths lesson as Uncle Anwar sat at the *sofra* with us. I made sure I made the least eye contact with him as possible during dinner, but unfortunately, I was sitting directly in front of him, so it was a hard task to maintain.

Bahba only had Uncle Anwar left from his family. He had lost his Bahba, Mother, and younger brother Qais in a landmine blast a few years ago. The three had been in the family car heading into town to get some supplies when the car drove over a mine. "The car blew up and flew up into the air like a toy and fell to the ground in a ball of fire, with shrapnel flying in random directions." I had overheard Bahba describing the tragedy to one of his friends one day.

Bahba used to tell us wonderful stories about

his two brothers during their childhood. But these stories didn't seem to resemble the relationship Bahba had with Uncle Anwar nowadays. Uncle Anwar was three years younger than Bahba, but they didn't seem to share the close bond that Imran and I had.

Maybe the grief of losing their family in the blast was too much for them to bear. Perhaps that's what happened when people got older, they grew apart? I hoped it didn't happen with me and Imran. Sure, we fought with each other, but I loved my brother dearly. He was my best friend.

* * *

That night I woke up in my bed. I was overheated, sweating and something heavy was on top of me. Opening my eyes, I could make out Uncle Anwar's face. Terrified, I wanted to scream but couldn't open my mouth. I lay there motionless, the realisation dawning on me that he must have stayed the night again. I began to cry softly.

"Shush, you'll wake everyone up," whispered Uncle Anwar, as I was now sobbing uncontrollably.

"Shut up! Stop making a scene," he said in an angry yet controlled tone. He jumped off from on top of me and zipped up his pants, ran out of the bedroom, and conveniently entered the main toilet next to my bedroom. My crying continued and got louder like I had lost all control over my emotions.

My wailing woke Imran whose bed was only a few centimetres from my bed. Even though he is a heavy sleeper he was now wide awake and trying to comfort me. Soon after Mother ran into my bedroom and turned the light on. She held me up from my shoulders and shook me as if to try and wake me up from a bad dream. Mother then held me in her arms to comfort me.

She then asked, "What's wrong? Did you have a bad dream?" My tongue felt heavy, I couldn't put any words together into a sentence and kept weeping uncontrollably.

"It's okay Zahra, it was just a bad dream, you're safe now," Mother said in a comforting tone. My entire body felt paralysed. I was finding it hard to breathe like a heavy iron bar was resting on my chest.

Chapter 5

"Come on you two, hurry up and zip up your suitcases. We must leave soon!" Mother shouted from the living room.

It was difficult to pack everything up in the one suitcase each of us was allowed to bring on the plane. Imran kept packing and removing items from his suitcase, not sure what to take and what to leave behind. But I knew exactly what I wanted to leave behind. I wanted to delete the memory, better yet forget the existence of Uncle Anwar all together! I decided not to refer to him as "uncle" anymore. It was an insult and tarnished what should be a beautiful relationship. He didn't deserve being referred to by any title used to address a man or even an animal! The only thing I could think of calling him in my mind was "It"!

As I sat in the taxi, I was dreading seeing "It" again at the airport. Bahba had mentioned earlier that he was coming directly to the airport as he lives close by. Thankfully he was just coming to farewell us and was not coming with us to Australia, at least not for now. *But what if he did eventually come to Australia to live with Bahba and our family?* The thought of the possibility of "It" being in the same country as me again made my stomach twist into knots.

We all sat on the blue chairs in the airport, waiting anxiously for our flight, having checked in our luggage. In the distance, I saw a familiar figure approaching. Instantly I got that sinking feeling in my heart and my stomach lurched again. It was a sickening physical reaction to seeing "It."

"It" approached the family, hugging and kissing everyone in the queue and saying goodbye, coming closer and closer to me. My body froze and my heart thudded fast in my chest. I started to sweat and couldn't breathe, my throat tightening. I could just make out a voice telling me, "Stand up and say goodbye, what's going on with you?" I stood, but immediately felt my legs weaken and give way.

When I opened my eyes, I was in Mother's arms, and she was splashing water in my face.

"There we go, good to have you back with us! It must be too early for you to be active, out of bed on an empty stomach," said Mother gently as she handed me a bottle of water to drink. "You gave us all such fright that's for sure, especially poor Uncle Anwar," Mother said with a slight giggle.

Bahba said that we were near the departure gate and only those boarding the flight were allowed to go through. A sense of relief came over me with the realisation that I had escaped from any interaction with "It." Knowing this, I finally felt a sense of calm and safety. Even though I had not actually been under any kind of attack, just seeing and being near "It" had been enough to cause the panic that took over me.

* * *

I stared out the aeroplane window, all the buildings and the landscape had become distorted the higher the plane rose into the air. The image through the plane window was becoming more and more like a mosaic as the plane got higher up into the sky and soon the plane was surrounded by cushions of fluffy clouds. I appreciated the beauty of God's magical creation from a bird's eye view. The skies above seemed so heavenly and magical. The fluffy plump pillows of perfection looked like they were handcrafted one by one—morphed into uniquely different shapes the more I stared at them.

I'm on a plane! Suddenly the realisation hit me and to my surprise I was really enjoying it. I wasn't confident when it came to heights. Bahba would take Imran and me to the state fair in Peshawar Mor and go on the amusement rides. Imran always wanted to go on the rides that are high up in the air like the Ferris wheel, while I preferred the ones that were closer to the ground, that span fast in a circular motion. Imran was a bit of a daredevil like that. He was not afraid of heights or new things, and he never shied away from a challenge.

"*Wah, wah,* this is so amazing! Can you believe that we are on a plane? Never thought we would ever actually experience this. I have only read about aeroplanes in our schoolbooks, but to travel in one is totally another thing!" Imran said with such wonder and amazement in his eyes.

I smiled back at him, feeling grateful for having him in my life and for this experience. As I turned back to stare out the window I hoped and prayed that the next chapters of my life were going to be great—filled with joy, good times and happy memories. I was filled with excitement at the prospect of seeing Aunt Inji again after so long. *Has living in Australia changed her at all?* I wondered.

Chapter 6

I ran into Aunt Inji's arms and hugged her. I felt a sudden lightness and calm come over me, as if my mind had somehow magically been wiped clean of all the negativity and toxins. I felt like the old "me," the untamed, free and innocent "me." Both crying and so happy to see each other after so long, we didn't know what to say or do. We just stood there embracing each other until Grandmother intervened cheekily and said, "Okay enough of that, it's my turn to hug Zahra!"

Grandmother separated us and held me in her arms. I could smell the rose water perfume that she always wore, the one that she got from Haj when she went to Saudi Arabia for the pilgrimage.

There were hugs in all directions, with laughter and tears in between. It felt surreal! All of us united again! I was floating on a cloud like those that we flew over earlier. I loved this warm, wonderful moment, after feeling alone and full of anxiety recently.

"I can't wait to take you to the shopping centre tomorrow and get you some nice clothes and toys!" said Aunt Inji with excitement and joy.

What is a "shopping centre"? I thought. *It must be where they buy things from, here in Australia.*

"You will love the beautiful Christmas decorations up at this time of the year. It is like our Eid celebrations but much more colourful and vibrant," Aunt Inji went on with sheer excitement.

What is Christmas? I wondered. I had so many questions floating around in my mind. I paused my mind for a moment and acknowledged where I was, so that my body and mind could unite and be there in that moment.

The car ride to the house was even more breathtaking. The beautiful Sydney weather and clean air refreshed me. I stared at the towering buildings and began to imagine my life here. *What will it be like?* One thing I was sure of was how beautiful this place was. Like a movie or a postcard, perfect whichever way I looked through the car window.

"Aunt Inji, do they speak our language Dari, or do they speak Urdu like they do in Pakistan?" I asked curiously.

"Neither, my *jhan*, they speak English! Don't

worry Zahra, you will pick up the English language very quickly. It's easy. If I could pick it up so quickly, you will do too once you start school," Aunt Inji responded with great encouragement.

A slight sense of worry filled inside me. *How will I communicate at school if I cannot even speak this language, English?* Aunt Inji had mentioned over the phone a few weeks ago, before the line had disconnected for the tenth time, that we as immigrants must work twice as hard to succeed here. Things were starting to feel real, and I knew that I had a lot of learning and adjusting to do, to get used to this new place.

I was so excited about this new beginning. I felt almost like being in a fairy tale and I was feeling extremely lucky at that very moment and filled with a profound sense of appreciation. It was like a beautiful mirage, so perfect and elegant.

As the wind blew in my face from the car window, I closed my eyes and let the breeze take me away to imagine a new life. It would be a safe and happy life, away from not only the traumas of war but also, you know, from "It." I hoped I would never have to see him or speak with him again.

"So, what do you think princess?" Aunt Inji asked as she flashed me a warm smile bringing me back to reality.

"I haven't seen anything like this before! It's so beautiful and magical. It feels like I'm in a dream and that I'll wake up at any moment," I replied excitedly.

"Wait until you see the beautiful beaches, the harbourside and the city, it is truly magnificent!" Aunt Inji exclaimed. She tucked her hair behind her ear, her hazel eyes glowing with enthusiasm.

"Back home in Afghanistan, and even Pakistan, we have lots of beautiful rivers; here they have the rivers too but also stunning beaches with beautiful aqua blue water that meets the golden coloured sand," Aunt Inji described in admiration.

I wondered what a beach looked like and what sand would feel like in my hands and in between my toes. My imagination tried to take over, tried to create images of golden beaches, but without any similar experience, I couldn't come close.

Chapter 7

It was 1991 in Australia and yesterday was my eleventh birthday. We'd had a small gathering to celebrate with the family. Mother had gone all out and created a feast fit for a queen. Unlike when we lived in Pakistan, time seemed to be passing by very quickly here. Imran and Bahba had gone to the butcher shop in the next suburb to get some halal meat for dinner, leaving Mother and I behind to do the usual Sunday chores around the house. After that, Mother went to pray.

She sat calmly on her prayer mat, both hands cuffed together, side by side, raised up in front of her as she finished her afternoon prayers. I loved watching Mother perform her prayers, because she seemed the most at peace in those moments. She usually wore her floral scarf when she was praying, pinned securely on one side of her head.

In that very instance, as I watched her in such a state of peace, I wanted to tell her everything. I wanted her to know my dark and shameful secret, about what "It" had done to me back in Pakistan. This was the reason for the nightmares I was having almost nightly, filled with fears that he might come back and hurt me again.

In the light of day, of course, I knew it wasn't possible to be hurt by him again, knowing that he was actually oceans away in America.

Soon after we had left for Australia, he had been granted a visa to emigrate to the United States. Bahba had mentioned that "It" had quickly accepted this opportunity, with the situation for Afghan immigrants in Pakistan deteriorating with police brutally targeting them.

I finally wanted this invisible wall between Mother and I to be torn down; I so desperately wanted to be closer to her. I longed for the kind of relationship where I could tell her everything, to indulge in secrets, to giggle ourselves silly about nothing. To share my joy and tears with her and to feel close to her. The kind of mother and daughter relationship I had read about in books and saw on TV.

"Mother, I want to tell you something," I said as I sat next to her on the floor and held her hands in mine. Her hands felt soft and smooth like silk. Mother gazed at me as a look of uncertainty and curiosity filled her eyes.

I told Mother everything about "It" and all that had happened in Pakistan. As I was talking, I could feel a sense of relief come over me, tears rolling down the side of my face. I felt like a cloud high in the sky, light and fluffy.

Tears rolled down Mother's face too, but suddenly she jerked her hands out of mine and stood up.

"Ya Allah," she cried out as she aggressively pulled her floral scarf off, causing the pin to fly off, ripping the side of it.

"Mother, Mother!" I screamed, crying as she walked away from me.

"I can't deal with this right now!" she said, pushing me aside and rushing around the house. She grabbed her handbag from the living room floor and strode out of the house slamming the front door behind her.

Mother had never left me or Imran home alone before. I felt scared and confused. I walked around the house anxiously wondering what to do. *Should I follow her outside? I hope she is okay!* My legs became weak and I needed lie down. I managed to get to my bed and lay there waiting for her as all kinds of thoughts raced through my mind. *Is Mother upset with me? Does she blame me?* All these questions flooded my mind.

While I wondered where Mother had gone, I lay still looking out the window at the skies above. *What agony it is to wait on someone,* I thought.

I often looked at the sky with wonder about its beauty and how it was always coloured perfectly with beautiful shades of blue and white—fluffy clouds that floated effortlessly. But at that moment, I was having trouble appreciating its beauty. My mind was overwhelmed and filled with worry.

Chapter 8

Looking at the sky, I felt closer to God for some reason, maybe such a beautiful creation made me feel nearer to its creator. Gazing at the slowly moving clouds I asked God for guidance in this confusing time in my life.

I had always spoken with God about everything, from as far back as I could remember. It's as if He could always hear me when I called on Him for strength and guidance. I had told Him everything about everyone in my life, my deepest thoughts—even about "It," because God and I had no secrets. Speaking to God like this felt right, it gave me strength and I was sure that he would keep my thoughts and secrets hidden in the sky behind those large floating clouds. But on this day, I was gazing at the sky with anxiety and deep worry.

Then I heard the door lock click open. I jumped out of bed and walked towards the entry door to see if Mother had returned. She stood near the door, very still with a distressed and disappointed look on her face; eyes bloodshot red like she had been crying the whole time she was away.

"Why didn't you tell me about this earlier?" Mother asked in a sharp angry tone.

Before I could answer her, she asked, "Does anyone else know about this?"

"No, I haven't told anyone about this I promise," I replied in a shaky voice, not really knowing what to expect.

"That night in Pakistan when you were crying, after I came to comfort you because I thought you'd had a bad dream, I saw Anwar exit the bathroom next to your bedroom. At the time I thought it was a coincidence, but now I know it wasn't. Why didn't you say something that night?" shouted Mother.

I opened my mouth to reply but Mother went on angrily, "Did you enjoy it? Is that why you have kept this to yourself all this time?"

My heart sank deeper as I felt a sweep of heartache come over me like a typhoon. My throat tightened up like I had a rope around my neck, being pulled tight.

"You make me sick, you dirty girl! It doesn't surprise me that you are a dirty *faisha* from such a young age. I could see it in your eyes that you're going to turn out like this, a disappointment!" Mother threw her handbag on the sofa.

I had heard the word *"faisha"* before, but I don't know what it means. I know it's a bad word that Imran and I are not allowed to use. I remember the first time I heard this word was back in Pakistan when my neighbour Aunt Sarah's seventeen-year-old daughter, Fatima, ran away with some boy from the neighbourhood. Now Mother is using this bad word to describe me.

"That girl has brought nothing but shame to her family's name," I recall Grandmother saying to Mother about the scandal.

"That *faisha* has betrayed her family's trust and honour and is giving the rest of the girls in the neighbourhood a bad name," I remember the women from the neighbourhood saying to each other during their regular evening walks.

My heart started to pound fast like it was going to jump out of my chest. All the while, Mother went on hurting me with her words, but inside me it was like a huge physical pain. The realisation hit home that I had just given Mother more pain and another reason to dislike me.

Tears rolled down my cheeks as I stood in front of Mother shivering. *Maybe Mother is right, maybe what happened with "It" is all my fault!*

"Stop the acting with those fake tears you *faisha!*" Mother moved towards me and slapped me hard across the face. "I'll give you a reason to cry," she repeatedly slapped me until I fell to the ground screaming and crying in pain.

Mother grabbed my wrist, pulled me to my feet and dragged me to my bedroom. Throwing me on my bed, she slammed the door shut.

Now I wished I had never shared my secret. What had I done?

* * *

When I opened my eyes, it was nearly dark; the sun had disappeared into the sky and there sat the moon with a greyish stain, adding to its beauty.

I wondered why Bahba hadn't come to get me or check on me. A few minutes ago I had heard Bahba say, "Should I check on Zahra, maybe now she feels well enough to join us for dinner and have something to eat?"

I could hear Mother, Bahba and Imran talking along with the occasional clatter of spoons on plates. The sudden realisation of the afternoon's events came flooding in, Mother's anger and slaps now fresh on my mind.

"No let her sleep. I gave her some syrup to get rid of the fever, She now just needs to sleep it off and should be fine in the morning," Mother said in a low tone.

Why was Mother saying this? I was not sick, nor did I have a fever.

I lay there feeling confused and sore. It didn't seem as if Mother has told Bahba. Mother had not given me the chance to explain what happened and how I was feeling. I had wanted her to know that I had been too scared and confused about what had happened to tell anyone.

I was not the horrible person she thought I was. I thought I had been doing the right thing by telling Mother what happened. But now I wasn't too sure. I didn't think I knew what the right thing was anymore.

I wondered if Mother had told anyone or would tell anyone. *What if she tells Aunt Inji? I don't want her to hate me too.*

Chapter 9

The bright light of the sun cast a long shadow across my face as I lay in bed. I opened my eyes to let the early warmth of the sun's rays to embrace my skin. I turned to my side to shift the bright light away from my eyes. I looked out the window and gazed up into the beautiful summer sky. I suddenly felt something jab me in the eye, with my instant reaction to shut them tight.

It was Mother, I think she stabbed me in the eye with her fingers.

"It's 6 a.m., why aren't you still asleep? Are you waiting for your Uncle Anwar to come and pay you a visit?" Mother asked sarcastically.

My attention snapped away from the sky and back to reality as Mother's eyes bored into mine. I had learnt by now not to respond in any way, because if I did that would lead to more beatings and hurtful taunts.

Mother left the room, closing the door behind her. I lay there wondering whether her behaviour towards me would ever end. Right now, I couldn't see how it could end, unless I was no longer alive. Her words felt like daggers in my heart each time, leaving a trail of hurt following by numbness in preparation for the next attack. Mother's venom-filled words were becoming engrained in my mind and dominated the way I thought about myself.

But despite this, I did have some strength within. I resolved to win her back. I had to convince her that there was so much good still in me and that I was more than what "It" did to me. My plan was simple, to stay on the right path and be a good Afghan girl, who always did what she was told, and helped with the household chores. I would study hard, succeed at school and go to university. Maybe then she would see the good in me, maybe even be a little proud of me instead blaming me and feeling ashamed of me.

I drifted back into fantasy, deep in the sky behind the inflated clouds where I felt the most love. I asked God to never stop loving me, otherwise I would lose the ability to live. I lay in bed a while longer until it was time to get up and get ready for school.

I sat at the dining table in my maroon and blue high school uniform, which was quite different from last year's year 6 uniform of dark blue on light blue. The intricate maroon lines added a new dimension to the plain blue in the background.

I placed the bowl in front of me and filled it with a handful of cereal and poured enough milk to just cover it. I forced the spoon into my mouth and chewed resentfully. In Australia, breakfast was different. We no longer sat around the *sofra*—Bahba, Mother, Imran and me. Neither did we have warm Afghan bread fresh from the bakery with paneer and sweetened green tea. It was rushed and not as intimate as it used to be. I just wanted to finish the morning routine and head off to school. School to me had become a safe place to escape from Mother's daily taunts and hurt.

But although school was "safe," it had its own challenges. There were many diverse groups and each group tended to hang out together. It was a survival of the fittest situation. Otherwise, the choice was—a cowardly one, which I happily adopted—to keep my head down, keep walking and under no circumstances bring attention to myself or make eye contact with anyone.

The bus ride home was another war zone where it was a struggle to find a seat. If you were left standing then you had to hold on tight because the bullies on the bus fed off small shy girls like me, like lions enjoying the hunt.

Imran's school experience, on the other hand, was in stark contrast to mine. We were at the same school but I didn't usually see him. He was always busy with his group of friends, laughing and clowning around. Being a popular kid with his witty charm and outgoing personality, Imran enjoyed high school.

I wished I could be more like him, careless and free, living life as a high school kid should. He was doing well in school, had lots of friends and even had a part-time job at Kmart. If he was asked what he wanted to do when he finished high school, he would say, "Only time will tell!" and burst out laughing.

I had picked up the English language quickly and was able to read well, but speaking was still daunting. I was working really hard on my accent so I could sound more "Oz". Mother didn't allow Imran and I to speak English at home, but we still did when she wasn't paying attention. It just felt more natural now to speak in English instead of in Dari. We'd sometimes whisper in English or close the bedroom door, so Mother didn't hear us.

In spite of my progress in English, maths

was another matter altogether. Just entering the maths classroom caused a bodily response in me. I sometimes got intense heart palpitations, with my body feeling as if I had dumbbells on my chest and I'd have trouble breathing. It was beyond my control and even if I didn't feel it physically, my mind would go into a kind of fog. Sometimes I wondered if it had anything to do with the incident when "It" was left in charge to "help me" with my maths homework. *I think I'm damaged and I don't know what will fix me.* Whatever the reason, I was falling behind.

So when I was offered extra support from my maths teacher, Mrs Wilbert, I accepted gratefully and I'd stay behind after class. I liked Mrs Wilbert's teaching style and with her extra help I started to do well, even above average during the exams.

Not being able to speak about what had happened made life hard sometimes. I still hadn't told anyone except Mother. I wished someone knew who understood me and the pain, hurt and the confusion I felt. I had trouble trusting people, especially men, whether they were a teacher or a family friend.

Most of the time I was surrounded by people, my family or classmates but even so, I felt very lonely. And the recurring nightmares haunted me every night.

So school and home were lonely places for me but at lunch time at least I had books. They would never let me down! My love of reading was only getting stronger as my English improved. Through reading I could experience happiness and feel what it was like to be loved. I read as much as I could at school, on the way to and from school and at home, whenever I could. Books felt like an escape, like entering a time machine and being transported to a fantasy life.

This was especially so when I started to read books with more words than pictures, what they referred to in Australia as a "novel." I didn't think pictures were needed when you could read your way into fantasy, creating your own mental images.

The other joy of my life was Aunt Inji! Although she was super busy with her studies, and I didn't see her often, when we did get together it was so amazing. I wasn't sure if I could have survived life if it wasn't for Aunt Inji's love and support.

Chapter 10

"Hurry Up! You'll be late," Mother shouted.

"Yes Mother," I replied, grabbing my school bag and hat and heading for the door, while she waited impatiently near the mailbox. Imran passed Mother and started to walk towards the bus stop.

I quickly walked towards Mother but before I could say a word her fist swung towards me and struck me straight in the stomach.

Winded, I gasped for air. I should not have been shocked, as some form of abuse from Mother had become part of my morning routine. But the element of surprise was always there as I never knew when or what was coming. Whether it was a hurtful comment, a swing of her wrist or an aggressive pull of my hair, I always had something nasty to endure.

After telling Mother about "It," her dislike of me had grown even more. I'd learnt to mentally disconnect from her toxic daily behaviour in the hope that it might help her release the hate she has bottled up inside for me and maybe one day learn to forgive me, maybe even love me again.

Mother was incredibly cunning and never abused me in front of Bahba or Imran or in front of her friends or other family members. With them she was pleasant towards me, which really messed with my head. She knew it was wrong—she would have been embarrassed if other people had known about it—but she didn't care what this hypocrisy was doing to me.

It was crazy but I'd got used to the daily abuse from Mother. I think I would been more worried if she didn't hit me, pinch me or pull my hair every morning before school. At least I knew she was demonstrating some form of emotion towards me. Every day she would find something to pick on to remind me that I was a *faisha*, to remind me of the nightmare caused by "It," to remind me that I was damaged beyond repair.

The beatings didn't bother me as much as her words. The bruises healed in the way that the sky recovers from a cloudy day or thunderstorm, looking beautiful and brilliant again, waiting for the next storm to strike. But Mother's words were on another level. Every day she would say something nasty, like she wished I was dead or she hoped that I would get run over by a truck. That I was so ugly that not even a dog would marry me. It was like an insidious infection worming its way into my mind and I was starting to believe it.

"Hurry up! Looking at your ugly face ruins my day. Look at that ugly nose—it reminds me of cat's paws—so flat and unattractive. And you're always daydreaming and making both of you late for school," Mother said angrily.

It took several minutes, but I finally managed to recover from the punch. I was gasping for something which I always took for granted, a simple breath of air. I rushed out crying and started to feel moisture run down the side of my cheeks. Slowly my breathing was starting to become more natural.

"There is no need to make a scene. You look uglier when you cry anyway!" Mother said.

Does my nose really look like a cat's paw and is that an ugly thing to have one's nose look like? Who gets to decide what is beautiful or what is ugly? I wondered. I couldn't remember what my nose looked like or what a cat's paw looked like. But Mother was right, I was ugly and I felt ugly on the inside as well. *Maybe I have an ugly soul and that is why I feel this way!*

Thinking about my face, I remembered how I avoided looking at my own reflection. I couldn't look at myself in the mirror anymore. Perhaps it made me feel less alive or real if I avoided my reflection.

I wondered whether Mother had told Bahba about what happened to me in Pakistan, with "It." I was sure she hadn't told him, as Bahba's treatment of me hasn't changed at all. It would have broken Bahba's heart to know that his own flesh and blood could have done something so vile. I was glad Mother had kept my dark secret to herself. I didn't want Bahba to die of shame because of me or look down at me like I'm a *faisha*.

To my dismay, Mother still had occasional contact with "It" and so did Bahba. They were in touch with him over the phone often and spoke about their experiences in their new countries and reminisced about the good old days.

The fact that Bahba did still talk to his brother surely meant that he knew nothing. I felt so certain that if he did know, he would have cut "It" out of our lives for hurting me.

What bothered me so much was why I was constantly reminded that I was a *faisha* by Mother, when "It" was treated as if he hadn't done anything wrong at all. It was as if I was the only one to blame—that it was my fault! Where was his accountability for what he did to me? Or were men never held accountable for anything they did?

In an ideal world, I imagined how Mother would stand up for me and support me in solidarity against my abuser—"It." I would fantasise about Mother confronting "It" about what he did and beating him up with her bare hands till he cried and asked for forgiveness. In the process he would explain the reason behind his unconscionable behaviour. I imagined getting the justice I deserved for my pain; with Bahba finding out what happened and being devastated. He would call the police, "It" would be taken away and the judge would impose the full extent of the law on him! *Did that kind of justice ever happen?* I wondered. *Maybe it did for the lucky ones but I can't see that happening for me!*

After the punch, I stumbled past Mother towards the bus stop. Mother gawked at me like I was nothing until the bus arrived.

"Have a good day son," she said to Imran, kissing him as he stepped onto the bus.

I dropped my head down as low as I could and wiped away the tears as I got in, feeling a sense of relief as I found an empty seat and collapsed in it, thankful that the morning ordeal was over at least for now.

Chapter 11

I felt a warm gentle kiss land on my forehead as I slowly opened my eyes.

"Hello, my sleeping beauty," Aunt Inji said as she scooped me up and hugged me tight. "What are you doing sleeping in the middle of such a gorgeous sunny Sunday?" She took the book from my hand and gently pulled me upright.

"I was reading the novel you gave me and must have dozed off," I replied still half asleep, squinting to adjust my eyes to the light.

Exhausted after doing the usual chores for Mother, I'd fallen asleep whilst reading. I had cleaned all the toilets, vacuumed the house, hung out the clothes, washed the dishes and changed Imran's bed sheets and mine. Mother gave me everyday chores, but there were always more on the weekends.

I smiled at Aunt Inji as she sat in front of me with big, bright excited eyes, talking about how we should spend our day.

"How about I take you to Parramatta and we can catch up over some ice cream by the river?" she asked excitedly.

I nodded in agreement as she dragged me out of bed to get ready.

I quickly put on my jeans and a t-shirt. The excitement of spending an entire day with Aunt Inji, away from this house, was overwhelmingly thrilling. I ran down the stairs into the living area where Mother was sitting at the table. Aunt Inji was drinking green tea with her.

"You know you don't have to take her out and spend money on her, you can stay here, and I can make you both something nice to eat," Mother said as she took a sip of her tea before placing her teacup back on the table.

Intense disappointment took over me with the thought of Mother not letting me go out with Aunt Inji. I desperately wanted to get out, even for a few measly hours. I was like a caged pigeon needing to taste freedom, even if it was only temporary.

"I know dear Sis, but I want to take Zahra out on a special day, just her and me. I haven't seen or spoken with her for over a month! You and I have our weekly coffee schedule, but I want to catch up with my princess Zahra. I promise I will bring her back in one piece," Aunt Inji said as she giggled.

* * *

While I sat in the car next to Aunt Inji I felt safe. I could smell her sweet floral perfume and wanted to take it all in, as she excitedly spoke about university life and her studies. I wanted to soak up her positive vibes and gentle, caring nature.

She was the only one who really acknowledged me, understood me and believed in me. I looked up to her more than any other woman in the world. Aunt Inji was in her final years of medical school and I was so proud of her. She was such an inspiration to me.

For as long as I could remember, her dream was to become a doctor and help others. Her number one passion in life was education—especially educating women back home in Afghanistan.

She would say to me, "To educate a woman puts the wheels in motion to educating the world. Many people don't realise this, but us women, if given the opportunity, we can run the world. After all God has raised women's status in Islam so high that paradise lies under her feet, in her role as a mother. Bringing peace and unity in this world is a piece of cake if we ensure all women have access to education!"

I loved it when Aunt Inji spoke so passionately

about her beliefs.

Mother was also supportive of women getting an education but not with the same burning passion as Aunt Inji.

"Okay, enough about me. Tell me angel, what's going on in that pretty head of yours?" Aunt Inji asked suddenly catching me off guard.

Aunt Inji was the only person who called me "angel," and I just adored it. *But what if she knew the truth about me? Would she still think I was an angel?*

"Ahhm what do you mean?" I asked nervously.

"Angel, you don't seem yourself. You seem lost in thought and withdrawn most of the time. It's been bothering me for a while, but I haven't found the right time to ask you. Is everything okay?" she asked, genuinely concerned.

My heart began to pound rapidly in my chest. "No, no I am fine you just haven't seen me in a while that's all." I began to panic inside. *Does she know about "It"? Has Mother spoken to her about me? I couldn't bear her being disappointed in me too if she found out about my terrible secret.*

"Are you sure? You know I'm here for you if you need to talk about anything. I mean it," Aunt Inji said gently.

Part of me wanted to hug her and tell her

everything—to clear my chest and free the caged Zahra forever. She might have been able to help me make sense of what happened and Mother's treatment towards me. On the other hand, I knew that telling Mother had brought so much misery into my life on top of having to deal with the never-ending flashbacks and nightmares. I couldn't bear losing Aunt Inji's love and respect, like I had with Mother.

"I know. You've always had my back and supported me. Thank you," I said. I felt a warmth spreading through my heart knowing that she loved and cared about me.

"Listen here you, just focus on your studies. Work hard at school and I promise you it will pay off because uni life is wonderful!" She lifted her head happily, tossing her long curly hair away from her face.

"I don't think I am smart enough to get into uni like you, but I'll try and finish year 12 for now and see how I go," I said as Aunt Inji pulled over and parked the car.

Aunt Inji turned and stared straight at me as she pulled out her keys from the ignition. "You listen to me, and you listen well! I don't want you to ever say that you CAN'T do something in life ever again, you hear me?"

She continued with mixture of encouragement and excitement, "Even if everyone else around you says it, you don't! You are such a smart and beautiful young girl, and I believe in you and know that if you work hard, you can achieve what your beautiful heart desires. Who knew I had it in me to get into Med school here in Australia, but I did it—with lots of hard work of course!

"You must believe in yourself. If you don't, then no one else will," Aunt Inji continued, her eyes suddenly welling up with emotion.

I looked into Aunt Inji's beautiful hazel eyes and smiled as tears filled my eyes too and hurried down my cheeks like an overflowing stream. *No one has ever called me beautiful or smart in my entire life! I don't care if it's true or not. Feels so wonderful to hear such kind words, but even better is the realisation that someone loves me enough to believe in me so much. Believes in me more than I could ever believe in myself!*

"Oh angel, please don't cry. I didn't mean to make you emotional," she said as she put her arms around me in a delicate but sweet embrace.

I felt safe for the first time in so long.

"Don't worry, these are happy tears. Thank you for believing in me, it means so much to me," I managed to say through the flow of tears.

"Okay enough of these tears, let's go and make the most of our time together!" she said as we got out of the car.

We spent the rest of the day wandering along the riverbank, then watching the beautiful sunset that began to form on the other side of the river. It was like a canvas filled with a pool of dazzling colours of yellow, red, orange and purple. I had never seen anything more beautiful and breathtaking as the toasted Australian sunset.

Chapter 12

Several years had passed since I started high school, yet it had the same old charm!

"Go back to where you came from, you import!" Melissa shouted at me from across the table as she stood up from her seat.

Melissa was a tall well-built Australian girl with beautiful blonde hair like the colour of the sun when it makes a full appearance in the afternoon. She had gorgeous blue eyes like the sea that lapped the beautiful beaches surrounding this picturesque country. She was always busy writing notes to others in class and didn't care much for her studies.

I had just asked her to have her draft group work assessment task ready by tomorrow for English so that we could go over it as a group and make sure everything was in sync before handing it in on Friday, when she launched her attack on me.

It was obvious that Melissa didn't like me and her hurtful words, calling me an import, proved it. I first noticed her reaction when I sat next to her in the year 9 intermediate English class earlier this year, when she pointedly ignored me. I considered myself an Australian–Afghan and I so wanted to belong, but when people said hurtful things like that I felt like an outsider. I was just as much an "Oz" as she was, except I didn't have blue eyes, blonde hair, and porcelain skin.

Firstly, this was Aboriginal land, I recalled from history lessons in year 8 and that needed to be fully acknowledged. Secondly, this nation was built on multiculturalism.

I wish Melissa had sworn at me, as it would have hurt less than calling me an import and telling me to go back to where I came from. Unfortunately, comments like this had become something of the norm to me in high school. Even though coming to school was an escape from the ordeal at home, it too was a battlefield with its own kind of warfare.

I was the shy, foreign girl in class who always had her head buried in a book. The dull girl, a "plain Jane" was the term I imagined others might use to describe me. I wondered what my reflection in the mirror was like and what people thought when they saw me. It probably wasn't attractive. Maybe that was why no one had approached me or had wanted to get to know me.

I still couldn't look at myself in the mirror—my reflection made me feel uncomfortable. Maybe my appearance made others uncomfortable as well.

The last time I looked closely at myself in the mirror was at Grandmother's house when I was around four years old. I loved her tall, white, free-standing vintage mirror with beautiful wood carvings around the edges. I recall spending hours staring at my small figure while trying on Grandmother's collection of scarves.

The unfairness and cruelty of Melissa's comments caused something to snap inside me. My blood was boiling as I stood up and faced her straight on and unleashed my wrath. "Believe me I would go back this minute if it wasn't for the war raging back home, in order to get away from insensitive and rude people like you. You spoiled brat!"

My heart was pounding as I stood frozen on the spot. It was like I had been possessed so deeply with anger that I had lost control and just blurted out those words. I couldn't even remember what I had said.

I had now unintentionally captured the entire class's attention and all twenty-five pairs of eyes were staring at me and Melissa, transfixed with their mouths wide open in shock.

I managed to conjure up enough strength to walk out of the classroom, bursting into tears along the way. I sat on the steps near the library as I nursed my aching heart, which revealed its pain through irrepressible tears.

I looked up into the clear summer sky and spoke to God as I always did. I questioned him, *Why I am at the receiving end of pain and hurt wherever I go in life? Is this your way of testing my patience?*

Just then, a sympathetic voice cut in, "So here you are. I've been looking for you everywhere."

It was my English teacher, Mrs Reed. She sat next to me and gently wrapped her right arm around me. She was the kind of teacher whom every child would want. She was passionate about teaching, loved children and her lessons were always an adventure. She made learning fun and reminded me of Aunt Inji in so many ways.

"You know, people sometimes say silly things in the heat of the moment and don't really mean it," Mrs Reed said softly as she continued to squeeze my shoulders.

I nodded in agreement, trying to fight away the tears.

"You are a wonderful person and just as much an Aussie as any other person in this country. Don't let anyone tell you otherwise," she said fervently.

I couldn't help but smile back at her.

"Now that's the way. I'm glad I managed to get a smile out of you. You are a highly intelligent young lady—don't you ever forget that." She gently removed her arm from my shoulders.

"Life is too short to hold a grudge. Maybe give Melissa another chance? She too is terribly upset about what happened. What do you say champ?" Mrs Reed grinned at me.

I managed to nod in agreement and gave a smile to reciprocate hers. Mrs Reed then sympathetically reached out both arms and hugged me.

* * *

That night I lay in bed processing the day's events. Of course, I didn't tell Mother about what happened. I had decided not to tell her anything unless I really needed to. I had learnt that telling Mother didn't help me in any way, in fact it created more problems for me and made life more difficult for her.

Today, Mrs Reed made me realise that being strong was the only choice I had in life. I would make Mother proud of me, study hard and become the person she could learn to love. I'd show her that I was more than what she thought of me—a *faisha*—I was so much more than that.

Mrs Reed's positive words were the motivation I needed. At home Mother always spoke about Imran being intelligent, that he would make it to university, raise the family name higher and make them proud. I agreed with Mother, Imran was bright, getting top grades for nearly all his subjects at school. He was someone I would forever look up to along with Aunt Inji.

But I never heard Mother talk about me in that way, even though I got top marks in some subjects. I knew I wasn't as smart as Imran but I would change that and work harder, study harder and make something of myself. I would win her back, even if that was all I did in life. I would read Mother's mind and do what she wanted without her saying a single word. Then she would have no choice but to accept me and love me again.

Chapter 13

I poured a glass of freshly brewed Afghan green tea for Mother while she sat at the dining table and continued to argue with Bahba, while Grandmother sat there casually sipping hers.

"No amount of money will ever be enough for you! We are not back home where I made lots of money and lived rent free. Do I have to remind you that we are in a foreign country where I can barely speak the language, let alone make good money?" Bahba asked in frustration.

"It's not my fault you're inadequate and can't provide for your family," Mother replied scornfully.

Bahba had been a successful businessman back in Afghanistan. He had imported goods from around the world and sold them on the streets of Kabul. Grandmother always said that Mother's star began to shine brightly when she was arranged to marry Bahba.

"Your Mother was only about your age, a teenager, when she was arranged to marry your

Bahba. Your Mother had no idea what her future husband even looked like," Grandmother said to me. "Oh, it was such wholesome fun to tease your mother about her future husband!" Grandmother was reminiscing cheekily as Mother and Bahba continued to quarrel in the background.

"As soon as I showed your mother your Bahba's photograph, that was it my dear girl, love began to blossom in your mother's eyes like roses blooming fully in the beautiful spring air," she said.

"In fact, from memory, your mother snatched the photo out of my hand and gazed into it before pressing it against her chest. Then she raised her head to see whether I was watching her. Caught one glimpse of me before she giggled shyly and ran into her bedroom with the photograph. Love at first sight is what it was, my dear girl!" Grandmother lovingly recalled.

I couldn't understand that. How could someone want to marry without knowing the person or seeing the person in real life? *Arranged marriages are such a barbaric act,* I thought. *It is an arrangement of hearts without the hearts really being in charge or in control.*

"Your Bahba was a very handsome and successful man back home," Grandmother continued before I interrupted her.

"What about Mother, what was she like?" I asked excitedly.

"Well, where do I begin?" Grandmother said as she placed her hand on her chin. "Your Mother had long, silky hair, a beautiful tall body shaped like an hourglass—spectacularly proportioned—and a charming smile that suited your Bahba's witty personality!" she replied proudly.

"She had a trail of men asking for her hand in marriage due to her beauty, but I wanted your mother to be with a man who respected her, treated her like a queen and took care of her," Grandmother said wisely.

"Your Bahba and Mother are very lucky to have ended up with each other because marriage is like a lottery—you either hit the jackpot, or you're left high and dry!" Grandmother said, bursting into laughter as she clapped her hands joyfully.

"That's the way it was done my dear, there was none of this love marriage nonsense that has no longevity." Grandmother made a facial expression of disapproval.

"Your Aunt Inji is next! She has several potential suitors, and we have narrowed it down to one young man and now I am left with the task of convincing her that it's time for marriage." Grandmother spoke as if it was mission impossible. "Then, my child, you're in line after that!" she whispered into my ear with a playful smile.

Aunt Inji getting married! How exciting! I thought. She would make a beautiful bride, not to mention a loving wife and wonderful mother. I prayed that she would be one of the lucky ones. I wanted a man like Bahba for Aunt Inji. Someone who was a gentleman, who would treat her well, take care of her and let her continue with her career as a doctor. Someone she could grow with in every sense of the word. My heart filled with excitement. I wonder what this young man looks like and what he does for a living?

Grandmother always told me that "woman was made from the rib of man," to be close to him and be loved by him. That's what the Quran said. I couldn't imagine ever getting married but if I did, it would never be an arranged marriage, I was sure of that! But as Mother often reminded me, "Who in their right mind would want to marry someone like you?"

However, I had noticed that Mother seemed to taunt me less often—usually it happened if I slipped up and hadn't done what she expected of me before she even verbalised it.

Anyway, men in general made me feel uncomfortable, whether it was Mr Foster, our PE teacher, or a total stranger at the shopping centre. The only man I could ever trust, love and respect was Bahba. I avoided talking to boys as it was, let alone getting married to one!

"Grandmother, I don't want to get married. Especially an arranged marriage, that's definitely not for me! It doesn't make sense to marry someone you don't know—a total stranger," I responded to her in protest.

"My child if you were in Afghanistan, by now you would not only have been married off but also you would have had a little one running around after you!" Grandmother said with a mischievous smile.

"Back home that's how it was. Girls married young and by their late teens, my child, they would have had a couple of little ones running around them, grabbing at their dresses," she continued.

Mother obviously overheard the conversation. "Yes, of course, you are too high and mighty, and above this tradition that has been around for so many years. What will you do? Smear our name in shame and marry for love? Those relationships don't last long once the lust is over, they then go their separate ways. Arranged marriages work and last the distance," she said angrily.

"I don't want to get married Mother—love or arranged. But I do think that the practice of arranged marriage needs to be gotten rid of and that two people who want to get married need to have spent some time together, getting to know each other's likes and dislikes before entering a lifelong commitment," I said, my heart pounding like it could bounce out of my chest out of sheer fear.

Mother glared at me, a deep furrow between her brows. I could sense the tension in the room suddenly rise.

"Mother, I respect this tradition—it has been in our community for centuries. It may have been the right tradition way back then but so much has changed in the world, and some traditions should evolve and change too, don't you think? Allowing men and women to be able to have a choice in who they marry is very empowering and liberating," I managed to scramble out.

Mother's frown turned into outright fury.

Grandmother must have noticed this, as she cut in, "Let it go, sweetheart, she is just a child. She doesn't know what she is saying."

Mother promptly stood and left the room

without a word, giving me the death stare all the way until she turned into the kitchen. It was kind of funny, but Mother's anger didn't scare me like it had when I was younger. Maybe it was because I was older and hopefully somewhat wiser, but whatever it was, she no longer hit me, at least she hadn't in the past few months. I was starting to challenge her more and stand up for myself. At the same time, I didn't want to upset Mother further than I already had or cause her any more grief. I tried to challenge Mother's thinking and opinion but in a very educated and mature way so that I didn't rub her up the wrong way too much.

An arranged marriage had worked well for Mother and Bahba, however. They were a good match. They got along well and didn't fight, unless it was over money, of course. That always seemed to come up—there was either not enough of it or Mother was overspending again.

I could see that Bahba was doing his best by doing any odd job he could get but it was tricky because he hadn't grasped the English language, even after many years living here. Mother didn't work outside of the house and she attended a TAFE English course while we were at school. It was eating up Bahba on the inside, not being able to provide as he used to back home. It used to be like he was a caterpillar making its way through a ripe apple! I just wished Mother would be a little more understanding.

Chapter 14

"What do you think, princess?" asked Aunt Inji as she stepped out of the car in her white dress.

I stared at her, my eyes wide, and I was quite sure my mouth was open too. It was like God had released a limited-edition angel to roam the earth on this one special occasion. The large bodice was made of exceptionally fine Italian silk and was hand stitched with sparkling Swarovski crystals. The long-sleeved lace added to the elegance of the gown. Her hair was worn up in a sophisticated bun topped with a Swarovski embedded crown, fit for the beautiful queen that she was.

"You look like a beautiful angel!" I managed to say as I got all emotional, seeing her in her wedding dress.

"Aww thank you sweetheart. You always know the right thing to say," Aunt Inji said as her eyes welled up with tears. "No, no. No crying today as my make-up will run like no tomorrow!" Aunt Inji said as she giggled slightly.

"Uncle Omar is a very lucky man indeed," I said as she kissed me on the cheek.

"Look at you my little princess, all grown up now. You look gorgeous in that dress!" she said admiringly as we walked towards the reception hall.

I was wearing a beautiful, fitted, emerald-green velvet dress, with long sleeves. Bahba had said, "That dress looks so good, it's as if it has been made especially for you!"

Everything with Aunt Inji and Uncle Omar had happened so quickly, skipping the engagement ceremony and going straight into organising a wedding. It was so fast that I hadn't had a lot of time to shop for a dress.

I had only seen Uncle Omar a handful of times and he seemed like a nice guy. He was a heart surgeon and extremely easy on the eyes. Ticking all the boxes—tall, dark and very handsome. They made a beautiful couple in terms of their appearance, level of education and with both being very successful in their careers.

Aunt Inji worked as a general practitioner at the local medical centre, and he worked in the cardiac department at a nearby hospital. Plus, Aunt Inji has seemed head over heels in love and happy since the engagement a few months ago.

This warm and fuzzy feeling didn't last long for me as I entered the reception hall knowing that "It" was going to be there too, having travelled from America with his wife and two-year-old son. My stomach was in knots as I dreaded the inevitability of seeing him again after so long. I was so worried about how that would unravel—not to mention the possibility of what he would say and do. Would he acknowledge what he had done or continue like nothing had happened?

I wondered, *Does he even understand how his vile abuse has impacted me terribly my entire life? Will he take ownership for his behaviour and perhaps apologise for the suffering he has caused me?* That would certainly allow me to have some sort of closure rather than pretending that the abuse was simply a cruel figment of my imagination.

I dropped off Aunt Inji in the bridal room, where she would get ready for her grand entry with Uncle Omar into the reception hall as a married couple. Then I went on to the reception hall, all the while feeling terribly ill in the stomach.

I hesitantly entered and, of course, the first face that my eyes fell upon was none other than that of "It"! Time suddenly seemed to stop. I could no longer hear the music and commotion in the background, but I focused entirely on the figure approaching me. I froze as he came closer and closer, accompanied, I assumed, by his wife and child in his arms, and with Mother and Bahba on either side of him.

"Hi Zahra, look at you!" he cried with joy and excitement. "You are unrecognisable! All grown up!"

I stood there, frozen like a statue, forgotten by time. I tried to say something, but no words came out. I didn't want to say hello to my abuser, not now, not ever! I managed to gather enough strength to turn around and walk straight out towards the exit doors into the fresh air, before my legs had a chance to give way.

Leaning on a handrail outside, I took a deep breath as the summer wind blew in my face.

What is Mother thinking? That I want to speak with him or see him? She must be out of her mind! I felt so angry that Mother had no clue how this whole thing had affected me and how much I was suffering inside. *I feel like screaming at the top of my lungs in rage!*

Even though it was a minimal quick glimpse of his face, I couldn't help but think that he hadn't changed much. *The same face, the same features—he hasn't aged a day!* I thought. He had put on some more weight, but apart from that, there was no other change that I could see. He did seem more upbeat than before, with his wife by his side and child in his arms, flaunting his happiness around for everyone to see! It was evident that life had been good to him. There was no ounce of remorse in his demeanour that I could see. *How dare he!* I thought.

I was no doubt going to hear about this from Mother and Bahba, and their disapproval of my behaviour towards "It." But I didn't care about that right now.

I kept holding the railing tight to ground me. I closed my eyes and continued taking in long, deep drafts of air—in and out—focusing entirely on my breathing. I had already known that "It" was in the country and had just got in from the airport that morning. A few days ago, I had overheard Mother say that "It" had booked accommodation at the Crown Plaza Hotel, knowing that we don't have spare rooms in our house. I had been so relieved that he would not be staying with us.

"Careful there, if you keep flexing your arms like that and squeezing so hard on the handrail you might just bend it out of shape!" a male voice said with amusement.

My eyes sprang open to find a young man dressed in formal attire, suit and tie. He was tall, with a medium build and had deep brown eyes and long dark lashes to match, which were quite captivating. I didn't think I recognised him from school or any family functions.

I let out a nervous laugh before asking, "Sorry, who are you?"

"My name is Humza. I'm from the groom side—you must be from the bride team," he said, smiling broadly.

My heart started pounding really hard in a wave of excitement and nerves. I couldn't explain the feeling simply because I had never felt this way before.

"I came out here to be alone and for some fresh air—can you please let me be?" I quickly said as he came closer to where I was standing. *I don't know why I get like this when it comes to the opposite gender. It's like I have no time for them even if he is being kind and is super handsome. Did I just mentally note that he is handsome?*

"I'm sorry, I didn't mean to invade your privacy. I just wanted to check if you are okay," he said softly. He took a few steps backwards before walking inside the reception hall.

What is the matter with me? Why am I so dismissive of men and unable to communicate? I don't even know the guy and am being so rude to him for no reason. He was being genuinely caring.

Imran suddenly burst out of the hall and appeared beside me. "Are you coming inside or are you going to spend the entire night out here? You're missing the all-important entry of the bride and groom," he said as he ushered me back into the hall where loud music had started up.

Aunt Inji looked divine, like an angel who had come down from the sky. She and Uncle Omar looked so good together. Such beauty—such a fantastic vibe in the room as everyone cheered their entrance together as husband and wife. It was just mind blowing. *I wish them both the best in their married life together!* I prayed inwardly.

I joined the bride and groom and the rest of the family on the dance floor to celebrate their union. As I jammed to a fast hip hop Afghan song with Imran, my mind wandered off towards the very handsome and charming Humza as he too was now on the dance floor. *Why would someone as handsome and sweet as him want to check up on me and talk to me? He seems like a really kind person,* I thought as our eyes occasionally met while dancing.

The thought of "It" was never far from my mind, now that he was in the same room as me! I tried to block his existence and tried to enjoy the party, but I couldn't help feeling overwhelmingly anxious in his presence. Meanwhile, Bahba and Mother were staring at me accusingly, still angry for my abrupt exit earlier and rudeness towards "It."

But how could he think he could casually approach me and talk to me as if nothing had happened?

Chapter 15

I sat at a desk in the large hall, my palms sweaty and heart pounding. I had known it would be hard, but I hadn't known it would feel like this. I stared at the test paper, face down on the desk, waiting impatiently to start my very first HSC exam. All the sleepless nights spent studying and stressing had all come down to this.

What if I fail everything? I can't handle another disappointment and cause Mother more grief! My plan to change Mother's perception of me and win her back would be doomed!

A voice rang out from the front of the hall, "You may begin by turning your English paper over. Reading time starts now. Good luck everyone."

Heart pounding still, palms even more sweaty, I turned the paper over and started to quickly read the questions. As I read and started to formulate the responses in my head, a slight sense of calm came over me. Realising that I had studied well and was prepared for these essay questions made the heart palpitations slow down to somewhat normal rate and my palms felt less sweaty. I closed my eyes after the 10 minutes reading time and sent up a small prayer thanking God for helping me and guiding me as always.

* * *

Walking out of the hall three hours later, my friend Marwa ran towards me and said, "That wasn't too bad, hey?"

I nodded as we hugged. "Isn't that a relief! I was so worried that I would stuff up the essay questions and get stuck! But with God's help I think we will be okay!"

I was so glad to have Marwa in my life. She was a kind and amazing friend. It had taken me a while to find a friend I really clicked with as she had just started at our school in the beginning of year 11. She was a beautiful soul, innocent and compassionate, and so smart considering she had only been in the country for a couple of years. *Afghan girls are so strong and so intelligent. They can turn any adversity or misfortune into an inspirational journey,* I thought.

I remember Marwa's first day at our school. I had been chosen by the year advisor, Ms Smart, to show her around the school. Marwa only spoke very limited English and with my ability to speak both my mother tongue, Dari, and English so well, Ms Smart had said, "You are the perfect candidate for the job!"

Marwa was shy and quiet at first but once you got to know her, her wit and sense of humour came through. Our friendship developed quickly, and we became study buddies and good friends. She was extremely focused and had high aspirations like me.

Coming from such a patriarchal Afghani community, a girl needed to stand out and make a name for herself, otherwise she'd get left behind in the kitchen, married off or just exist without any real identity.

I was lucky that I came from a family who allowed me to study. They wanted me to have aspirations and they supported my wish to attend university and have a professional career.

Whether they thought I could achieve all that was another topic all together. For Imran, it was expected that he would study hard and get a university degree but not so much for me. It was my job to prove them wrong, show them that I too could do what Imran was able to, and maybe even do better.

Marwa and I walked to the cafeteria, exchanging conversations about how we responded to each essay question. I sighed in relief, even if it was only a temporary respite until the next exam in two days. But I knew that the hard work and sleepless nights I had put in was paying off! I ordered the usual hot chips and energy drink and Marwa got hot chips with a Coke. Since meeting Marwa, school wasn't just an escape from home, or my past, but also an exciting and fun place where I could be myself in Marwa's company and share stories and aspire for the future as well.

I can't believe it! I've just finished my first HSC exam! It has been such a stressful lead-up to this day but there are more difficult days ahead, I thought as I sat there talking with Marwa. *Maths and Biology are just around the corner both on the same day within hours apart! I am going to need a miracle for this one to help me get through with flying colours. It is hard to comprehend that one's entire future hangs in the balance based on the outcome of this one exam!*

Chapter 16

"Please don't cry my love, everything will be okay. We are all with you and pray for things to change. Men usually step up and settle into married life once they become a Bahba," Mother said gently to someone on the phone.

I hadn't seen Mother so upset in a long time, crying quietly as she continued the call.

I washed the dishes patiently and waited until she had hung up and quickly asked, "Who was that Mother? Is everything okay?"

"It was Aunt Injilla, she's having some problems with her husband. Nothing serious or anything you need to worry about. It is common relationship stuff," she said shutting my concern and curiosity down quickly.

"Please don't do that Mother! I am not a child anymore. Did something happen to her? We need to help her if something is wrong," I said, surprising myself with my courage.

Mother did not respond in her usual passive

aggressive way, instead, still crying, she replied, "Her husband has been hitting her and not allowing her to continue to work outside of the home."

My heart sank so deep that I could no longer feel it beat in my chest. Then sense of rage came over me as I tried to process this news. "But he seemed like such a nice guy and agreed to all her conditions of her having a career and wanting to progress in her line of work before getting married," I said, feeling confused.

"That's men alright! They will say anything you want to hear until they get you where they want you, vulnerable and alone, then they strike," Mother said bitterly, wiping her face.

Then tears rolled down my own cheeks as I thought of Aunt Inji being hurt by Uncle Omar, along with all her dreams being crushed. Mother reached out to me and to my surprise grabbed me by the shoulders and hugged me tight. I couldn't remember Mother hugging me before. It felt uncomfortable at first but nicer the longer I remained in her warm embrace. We both cried together, my heart felt heavy with sadness for Aunt Inji.

"Omar has been hitting her and controlling her in many ways and even limiting her contact with us!

He wants her to stay at home and give up her job, which she is objecting to. How could he do this to her? We trusted him!" Mother said as she wept in my arms.

Aunt Inji had been married for only a few years; I wondered why we were only finding out about all this now. My mind was racing, and things were starting to fall into place. No wonder we had barely seen Aunt Inji since she got married and she hadn't even called me much recently. We had just assumed that she was really busy in her new life with her husband, all part of adjusting to married life.

"Mother, I have learnt at school about men behaving like this towards their wives. It sounds like Aunt Inji is experiencing domestic violence! We need to support her and get her away from this man. He could become extremely dangerous and could even kill her!" I was frantic with anxiety and worry.

Mother suddenly pulled away from me. "Calm down, no one is killing anyone! They are still newlyweds; it can take several years to adjusting to married life. I am not going to break up my sister's marriage! This is just a bump on the road for them to cross. Maybe if they have a child things might mellow down," she said.

Is Mother serious right now? What is she thinking? We need to get her out of there and help her stay safe.

"This is why I am so against arranged marriages!" I replied. "It's because they are two different people with different world views. They didn't know enough about each other before getting married. She deserves better!"

I knew this was not going to go down well with Mother as she was so set in her ways with her old school mentality, that anything remotely different was overwhelming for her.

"How dare you turn this around into something like this! Are you trying to pave a smooth path for yourself to love marriage, is this what this is about? Haven't you caused us enough shame?" Mother shouted angrily.

I stared her in the eyes with pain brewing in my heart. "No Mother, I have hated men ever since what happened to me when I was a child. This is not about me!" I exclaimed.

"I am just worried about Aunt Inji and the domestic violence she is experiencing, which seems to be extremely high risk based on what you've told me. We are lucky we live in a society where women have rights and choices, like leaving a man who hurts you. The law can hold them accountable for their behaviour, whether that man is their husband or their so-called uncle!"

I could see Mother's eyes widening with anger as I continued, "Another thing, you talk about shame, why is it that I am the only one carrying the burden of this shame on my shoulders for all these years, when I am the actual victim in this. I was a helpless, vulnerable, and innocent child!"

I went on, needing to get this out at last. "Where is my justice? Where were you when I needed you Mother? I needed someone to stand up for me and defend me but instead you broke me until there was nothing left but pain and shame. It's women like you who should be ashamed for not standing up for other women and their rights!" I said this in a raised tone of voice before realising I had gone too far. But it had been in my heart for so long like a script ready to voice, and I had finally said it out loud, right time or not.

Mother's face was frozen, with her mouth wide open. I don't think I have ever seen her speechless like that.

I didn't want to hear her reply because it would never be what I needed to hear from her. I managed to conjure up the courage to turn around and storm into my bedroom, slamming the door shut behind me. I knew the storm that was going to hit me after this would be turbulent. But I didn't care about that right now. I was shattered for Aunt Inji, she didn't deserve this. No one deserved to be treated like this from the person who promised to love them and take care of them.

Chapter 17

I hadn't known where to look. Aunt Inji's face was swollen, with a black eye on the left side of her face and some sort of red mark across her neck. She sat on the sofa next to Mother as she pleaded with her to let her stay with us until she could get her own place.

"My dear I would love for you to stay but I don't want to be responsible for the breakup of your marriage! You can stay here for as long as you need to, but then please return to Omar," Mother said sympathetically.

"Marriage takes time, and you need to be patient. I promise he will come around. Maybe have a child and that will change him and help make him a more responsible man," Mother said softly.

"That is the problem, you people don't understand. There might not be a next time! Look at me, take a good long look at the marks around my neck. He choked me, and this is not the first time, he's done this many times before," Aunt Inji said with desperation and sorrow in her voice as she pointed at her neck.

"I have lost count of the number of times he has choked me, and I've lost consciousness. Then he has apologised and bought me flowers, but then he would say that it was my fault for not listening to him," Aunt Inji was frustrated as she stood and paced back and forth.

"Why can't you see that having a child with him would be the worst thing I could do? That would tie me down with him for the rest of my life!" she sobbed.

I stood up and hugged her. "This is domestic violence! And it sounds like a cycle of violence, where you are walking on eggshells; constantly watching what you are saying and doing to avoid him getting angry at you. Then he can erupt at any moment over something very minor."

I held her at arm's length and continued, trying to convince her. "Then this is followed by the 'honeymoon' phase where he apologises and promises to never do it again. Yet he has gone through this cycle numerous times now. We learnt about this in personal development and health class," I said, hugging her again.

"You haven't even got your HSC results back and

you're already acting like you know everything, Miss Professor! Stop filling her head with nonsense. You are a child, what would you know about marriage!" Mother was angry and condescending as she glared at me with furious eyes.

"No, no, that is exactly how I feel, Zahra! I feel like I am trapped in a cycle that goes on and on, just like you said. I feel like I'm going crazy!" Aunt Inji said with realisation. "He tells me often that I am crazy and that it is all my fault. The worst part is that I was starting to believe him. It feels good to finally put a name to this rather than think I am losing my mind."

She continued, with a look of resolve on her face. "If this is what marriage is, then I don't want to be married any longer! My time with him has broken me. I don't know who I am anymore or what I feel. I put up with so much! You don't know half of what I have endured!"

Aunt Inji protested as she saw her sister's reaction to her words. "But this is where I draw the line. Stopping me from practising as a doctor is not going to happen! I have worked so hard to get to where I am in my career. No one can take that away from me!"

"But Injilla, do understand the gravity of what

you are saying? You want to be known as a divorcee?" Mother asked.

"My dear sister, I have put up with a lot in silence, but my soul is not able to endure any more of it! I'd rather that death was in my future than go back to that hell. If this is the kind of life you want for me, then send me back. I understand that you don't want to get involved and I respect your ideas about marriage and our culture," Aunt Inji pleaded, "And Islam is open to the possibility of divorce, and in fact that predates centuries in its practice of no-fault divorce. It's something the West has only recently discovered," she said in between her tears.

Mother leaned against the wall as she collapsed in a heap on the floor crying. "I didn't want this for you! You deserve happiness and love," she sobbed.

"I know and I want that too, but Omar is not the person who can give me that. He is not capable," Aunt Inji said. "I need some time to think straight and plan out what to do next. I knew this day would come. That's why I've been putting money aside, before giving him the rest of my pay. As head of the house he demands the money as soon as it arrives in my account," she let go of my embrace and turned to comfort Mother.

"Why does he take the money that you work so

hard for?" Mother asked, confused.

"Like I said sweet sister, you have no idea what I have endured for these few years. But I've done this to protect you all, for our family to remain respected in our community. I needed to save face and avoid the shame and guilt I feel for a failed marriage," she said broken heartedly.

"But no more! I am not an object to be sacrificed or used and abused like this. I am a woman yes, but that does not make me weak or a target for men like Omar." Aunt Inji's voice rose and her cries became louder.

Mother held Aunt Inji tight and comforted her. "My dear sister I had no idea you were in so much pain, and for so long. Please forgive me for not being there for you. I'm so sorry I haven't understood what you've been going through," Mother said with sincerity.

"I've made a lot of mistakes in my lifetime but know this, I am here for you. Whatever you need. I will stand by you, against our family and community." Mother wiped away Aunt Inji's tears from her face, handing her fresh tissues, and as she said this, she looked up at me.

I was shocked but pleased with the words Mother had just uttered so warmly to her sister. I felt that there was also maybe a small recognition on her part that she had not been there for me. Perhaps indirectly she was admitting that she had failed to defend me when she had known what "It" did to me when I was a child.

"You are so lucky and yet you have no idea," Aunt Inji said softly to my mother. "Your husband is the kindest and most caring man I know. More importantly, I hope you appreciate him. Nothing else matters—money, cars, career, they all mean nothing if he doesn't respect you as a person."

I lay in bed that night, trying to process the events of the day. I wanted to come to terms with what was happening with Aunt Inji and, most confusingly, why was she going through this? She was the kindest person I knew, so why was God punishing her like this? I remembered what the school *Mullah* once said in scripture class: "God tests you only so much as you are able to endure, and he tests those he loves the most even more."

Aunt Inji is a strong woman, patient and resilient. I know she will get through this with all of us by her side supporting her. I am not sure what her next step is or what she will even do tomorrow but I know she will get through this.

Chapter 18

Mother handed me some mail from the letterbox. It was a beautiful December morning, with the sun shining brightly in the clear crisp blue sky as I sat on the metal garden chair on the front porch. I went through the mail and placed the bills in one pile and handed them to Mother, with one letter addressed to me still in my hand.

Can this change the course of my life? Is this what I've been waiting for? It has to be!

"Who is the letter from? Is this the letter you have been waiting so impatiently for? To find out your HSC marks?" Mother asked inquisitively as she looked at the letter still in my hand while she carefully watered the plants.

"Maybe, I don't know Mother," I managed to say as I rushed inside the house and went straight to my room. This was the decisive moment for me. Had all the hard work and sleepless nights paid off or had it all been in vain? My heart was now beating fast in my chest and my hands were clammy as I sat on the edge of my bed mentally preparing myself for whatever was inside. I read the sender on the front of the envelope — University Admissions Centre.

My breathing increased its pace along with my heartbeat. I closed my eyes and prayed to God saying, "I surrender myself and my future to you, and whatever you have planned, as you are the greatest planner of them all." I ripped the envelope open and, in the process, I ripped the side of the letter as well, but it was still legible. I quickly skimmed through the contents.

My anxiety quickly turned into triumph as I read 99.1% allocated for my overall marks for the HSC! I jumped around in my bedroom, screaming with the paper in my hand and then burst into tears of joy. I was not used to happy news like this! In fact, this was the first time that I had received such positive news about anything. The relief that came over me was something else.

Mother and Aunt Inji entered the room with panicked looks on their faces. "What happened? What happened, is everything okay?"

I grabbed Mother by her arms and started to jump around with her and managed to rapidly say, "Better then okay Mother! I told you that I will make you proud of me and now I have. I have scored

99.1%! Do you know what this means? I can study any degree at any university that my heart desires!"

Mother was speechless. Aunt Inji grabbed me by the shoulders and hugged me tight and said, "Remember I told you, that you could achieve anything you wanted. Hopefully, now you believe me!"

I grinned at her and at Mother's shocked face that gradually developed into a smile as Bahba and Imran too rushed into the room. As I observed the vibe, it felt good to have everyone happy like this after so long. Everyone in the family has been so down and depressed lately with Aunt Inji's unexpected marriage breakdown. It was an even better feeling to know that this joy was because of my achievement.

Aunt Inji had been staying with us for a few weeks, and I loved having her there. Her presence had improved the family atmosphere, even though I wished it could have been under different circumstances that led her to live with us.

Aunt Inji chose to stay with us over Grandmother's house as Uncle Omar's family had been there a few times, demanding that she return to her marriage and make things work with her husband, and accusing her of abandoning her home.

This was such a joke! There was no acknowledgement or accountability of the wrong that Uncle Omar had done. The burden of making the "marriage" work was resting entirely on the woman in the relationship. The pressure on women in our community to stay in an abusive relationship and keep the peace was absurd!

Aunt Inji found a small two-bedroom apartment close to our house and was in the process of getting furniture for it. The place would be ready for her to move into in a week or so.

This was a bold step and I was so proud of her. She was an amazing role model to me and other young people in my community. Our culture was beautiful and so fulfilling, but at times it could also restrict us in so many ways. I knew that my family had a hard road ahead with the community looking down at us and criticising Aunt Inji for getting a divorce and living on her own. Unfortunately, just as Mother once labelled me, this would result in her being called a *faisha* in the community.

But if anyone could come out the other end even stronger, it was Aunt Inji. She was resilient and so positive and motivated. I looked up to her and hoped that one day I would be half the woman she was. I wanted to be independent and successful, and I never wanted to be dependent on anyone, especially a man! I would make sure that I had a career and was able to support myself. With such good HSC results I was no doubt one step closer towards this dream.

"Okay, time for a celebration cake," Mother said as she clapped her hands in the air to get everyone's attention. We all followed her into the living room to eat cake in honour of my results.

I was proud of Mother and how she was handling the whole situation with Aunt Inji. Knowing Mother, I honestly thought she would have a major meltdown and force Aunt Inji to get back together with Uncle Omar to save face in the community. But Mother was poised and she wasn't acting all crazy, crying or carrying on as she would have done in the past when dealing with a problem. She was being incredibly supportive of Aunt Inji and putting her first over her own name and reputation in the community, which was unheard of for her! I wish she'd had this wisdom and understanding back when I came to her with the abuse "It" inflicted on me.

Chapter 19

My stomach was in knots when I first laid eyes on the University of NSW campus entry gates for my first day of university life. I was super excited but petrified at the same time. This would be a life-changing chapter, requiring so much hard work and commitment.

I must have looked lost as I crossed the road to enter the campus gates. There was a long path that led towards large steps, surrounded by beautiful tall buildings on one side, and on the other side revealing a sizable field with luscious green grass, and tall cascading trees which provided ample shade. I was mesmerised by the sheer beauty and size of this place!

It's just so hard to believe that I am here among this intelligent crowd—a university attendee! I marvelled. *Who would have thought I had it in me? The young version of me wouldn't have even imagined being capable or even worthy of such an achievement.*

It was like being back at high school on my first

day, all over again! Not knowing anyone and feeling a mixture of anxiety and excitement. "Anxitement" is what I'd call it! Knowing that I was getting closer to my dream of becoming a doctor like Aunt Inji was exciting, but also terrifying.

Looking at my first-year timetable and campus map, I was able to find the building where I would be having my first lecture for biology. To celebrate this, I thought I'd get myself a drink from the cafeteria.

As I gazed at the menu—even though I knew I would get my usual energy drink—I could see in my peripheral vision a figure looking in my direction. I turned to see a handsome face staring directly back at me. I was shocked as I recognised his face, even though I couldn't remember where from. My palms started to get sweaty, and my heart was beating fast. You'd think I was competing at the school athletics carnival, in the middle of a 1 kilometre run!

"Hello, fancy seeing you here," he said as he approached me.

Then it suddenly hit me. It was the guy from Aunt Inji's wedding! The young man who came to check on me when I was having a panic attack after running in to "It"! He was kind and gentle towards me, asking if I was okay. I suddenly remembered that I had been so rude to him. *Maybe I can make it up to him by being friendly,* I thought.

"Hello," I managed to say as I tried to get the sweating and heartbeat under control. *Why does my body react like this whenever I'm in the presence of this guy?*

"I am that annoying guy Humza from a wedding we both attended a few years ago,"he said sheepishly.

It was a relief to put a name to the unforgettably handsome face.

"How long have you been attending this uni?" he asked with his hypnotic brown eyes gazing deep into mine, complemented by a beautiful smile that formed on his face.

"Hi Humza, nice to properly meet you this time. My name is Zahra. Well, today is my first day. What about you?" I pretended to casually ask like I didn't care but was just being polite.

"True story, it's my first day too!" he said as the smile converted into a cheeky laugh.

"Oh really? What course are you studying?" I asked and this time I was genuinely interested in the answer.

"Don't laugh but I am enrolled to study bachelor of medical studies, but time will tell if I am actually cut out to complete the degree and graduate," he said with a tone of self-doubt.

How could such a handsome and charming person like him have any self-doubt, I thought. *He is like a dream.* I tried to focus on the topic of conversation and endeavoured not to get lost in his gorgeous eyes.

"No way so am I! And why would I laugh?" I managed to say with a hint of excitement.

"Such a small world. What is the chance of seeing you here after all this time and both of us wanting to become doctors," he said sounding like destiny is at work.

Then it suddenly hit me. He must be related to Uncle Omar somehow! I recalled him saying at Aunt Inji's wedding that he is from the groom's side! The floral feeling inside of me suddenly disappeared into sudden clouds of darkness as all kinds of thoughts rushed through my head. I wondered, *Does he know about Aunt Inji's separation? Am I betraying Aunt Inji by speaking to him?*

"Well okay I better get going, I don't want to be late to class on the first day," I abruptly said. I lifted my bag and swung it onto my shoulder, without even getting the drink I had come for. I intended to get away from him as quickly as I could.

"We can walk up to the lecture hall together if you like. I have been told that for the first year of the degree, the timetable is the same for all students, so we have our biology lecture in ten minutes," he said as he walked beside me.

"Okay great. But I need to go to the ladies before the lecture, so I'll catchup with you later." I scurried away from him like he had a contagious disease.

I kept walking and did not turn around to see if Humza was following close behind or still looking at my direction.

I dashed into the women's toilet, reached the basin and quickly turned the tap on, running my hands under the cold water before gently patting my cheeks with my cold wet hands.

I am betraying Aunt Inji! How can I do this to the most amazing person in my life. What is wrong with me?

I took a few deep breaths, closed my eyes and composed myself and tried to come up with a strategy to stay clear of Mister Fluffy. I couldn't help but giggle to myself at the nickname I had just come up with. He was perfect—like a fluffy cloud—no flaws, just pure beauty and a mirage-like appearance.

Okay, enough of this silliness, I thought. *I need to pull myself together and get back out to the lecture theatre before I am late to my first ever lecture at uni!*

As I dried my hands and stepped out the door, I felt more relaxed and knew exactly what I needed to do. I headed down the busy corridor, students hurrying in every direction, towards the lecture theatre.

I had to ignore Humza and over time he would think that I wasn't worth being friends with and he'd leave me alone. I had bigger goals in life than worrying about handsome men and I needed to keep my eyes on the ball. Getting this course finished was not going to be easy, so I needed to stay focused.

Entering the lecture hall, the first pair of eyes to meet mine were none other than those belonging to Humza. He was waving frantically at me to get my attention. There was an empty seat next to him—presumably for me.

Why God, why is this happening to me? I like my boring life where no one pays any attention to me. I am like one of the background singers in a concert that no one notices because they are mesmerised by the main event.

I quickly looked away, pretending I was looking for someone and made sure I went as far I could in the opposite direction from Humza. I needed to make sure I put enough distance between myself and him. *I don't trust myself or my judgment when I'm around him.*

I sat down and didn't look back to where Humza was seated. I felt awful acting like that, all fake and pretending—it was something that I wasn't used to doing and I really wasn't like that! I hoped this would give him the hint that I didn't want to have anything to do with him. Knowing that he was from the same family that hurt Aunt Inji so much, meant I just couldn't think of being friends with him.

* * *

"How was the first day of uni, smarty pants?" Imran asked in a cheeky tone as soon as I entered the house.

"Yeah, it was okay. Very tiring but love the campus. It's so architecturally beautiful. Most of the students have super rich parents or are international students, but no surprises there."

That was all I managed to say to my brother as I headed into my room, dropped my bag onto the floor, and collapsed onto my bed from physical and mental exhaustion.

when I'm around him.

I sat down and didn't look back to where [illegible] was sat. I felt awful acting like that, all fake and pretending—it was something that I wasn't used to doing and I really wasn't like that. I hoped that would show him the hint that I didn't want to have anything to do with him. Knowing that he was from the same family that hurt [illegible] so much meant I just couldn't think of being friends with him.

"How was the first day at [illegible]?" [illegible] asked [illegible] cheerfully [illegible] as I entered [illegible] lounge.

"Really [illegible] but [illegible] the campus. It's architecturally beautiful. Most of the students I [illegible] international students [illegible] surprise [illegible]."

That was all I managed [illegible] as I headed into [illegible] and collapsed on my bed from [illegible] mental exhaustion.

Chapter 20

It was the morning and I was running late as usual. With the trains so often arriving behind their running time it would mess up my entire uni schedule. It also didn't help that I'd had a terrible sleep the night before with the usual nightmares about "It," before waking up in a pool of sweat. These were the same nightmares, occurring over and over, like groundhog day.

Will these awful dreams never end? I thought as I grabbed my bag and rushed out of the house.

Despite my haste, I paused as I went outside. The bright light from the Sydney autumn sun sprayed my face with sunshine and the cool breeze brushed my skin as I closed the door behind me. *What a blessing it is,* I thought, *to be greeted so pleasantly with such warmth. Like a warm hug on a winter's day, so comforting and satisfying.*

Running to my Chemistry tutorial, I entered the room like one hot mess. Quickly scanning the room, I searched for a seat to quietly and unobtrusively sink in to, but all eyes in the room were focused on my grand entrance. I was breathing heavily and my heart was thudding like a bass drum. Everyone must have been able to hear it in that quiet room. There was only one vacant seat and it was next to a familiar handsome face beckoning me towards it. Of course, it was Mister Fluffy AKA, Humza!

Out of all the people in the room, why does the only place to sit have to be next to him—AGAIN?

With all the pairs of eyes disapprovingly gazing at my direction now, including those of the tutor, I quickly made my way towards Mister Fluffy and reluctantly took the only place next to him.

"Hi. Lucky, I saved you a seat!" he gently whispered with a sensual smile that seemed to be permanently glued to his face.

"Hi. Yes, thank you," is all I managed to say in reply.

As the tutor continued with the lesson, I could feel my laboured breathing slowing. I imagined my cheeks and ears is turning pink now, as they usually do when I am embarrassed or feel shy. *I need to get my shit together! What is wrong with me?* I thought.

I took a few deep breaths, then pretended that I was sitting next to a stranger to try to get my body under my control again—and it was working! I could feel my shoulders starting to relax, my heart rate was returning to normal and I thought my flushed face was losing its rosy hue. I was off that Mister Fluffy train, at least for now.

I ignored him for most of the class and made little to no eye contact unless we had to pass around handouts from the tutor. The strategy was working for the moment, but how would I handle this moving forward?

This is meant to be the most exciting and fun chapter of my life and it's turning into a nightmare! I thought. *How can I get him to back off and leave me alone? My loyalty is always going to be with Aunt Inji!* But for now, I was plotting for a quick escape for when this class ended.

The trouble was, I had to admit to myself that I did like him. I enjoyed his company and I wanted to get to know him, but it would be unforgiveable to betray Aunt Inji by befriending Humza—someone from Uncle Omar's circle. I had already given my family enough reasons to be angry with me in this brief period of my existence, so I didn't want to add this to the litany of my crimes!

As the class came to an end, I hurriedly packed my things and made to leave. Then I heard him say, "Hey Zahra, a few of us first-years are getting together over lunch if you'd like to come?"

The way he said my name was beautiful to my ears. "Zahra." It was said so delicately. He made my name sound beautiful. *I really do have a lovely name,* I thought.

"I can't, not today. Need to head to the library for a bit," I said robotically, ignoring those distracting thoughts about the sound of Humza's voice and heading away from him.

"Oh come on, only for half an hour or so. It will give us all a chance to get to know the rest of the students in the faculty," Mister Fluffy said enthusiastically.

"Sorry not today, maybe another time," I said, thinking that there wouldn't be another time if I could help it!

"Okay then, catch you later I guess," he said disappointedly, turning back to the others.

I snuck a quick look back at him before leaving the room. He looked back at me too and dazzled me one last time with his mesmerising smile. I quickly looked away and left the room. *Why is he having this impact on me? What is it about him? It's never happened before. Whatever this is I need to get these emotions under control—by avoiding him all together.*

"How was your day?" Mother asked later that

night during dinner.

I was pushing the meat balls around on my plate, in a trance about the Humza situation. This debacle had taken over so much of my life that the situation at home with Mother felt insignificant. The only person who I could talk to about anything, is Aunt Inji but she was the one person that I could never share this with. I could only imagine the betrayal she would feel.

"It was okay Mother, just very tiring," I replied softly.

I wished I could speak to her about this. She might have had advice about what to do and the way I feel around Humza.

"Yeah, yeah, you're not a doctor yet, so don't get ahead of yourself. Remember you still need to help around the house even if you become a surgeon!" Mother said as she took her plate to the kitchen. "Quick come and help me with the dishes,"

Meanwhile, Bahba slowly lifted his head from the Quran and gave me a cheeky smirk before returning to his reading.

Chapter 21

Our usual family get-together happened every Sunday when we would all gather around the traditional Afghan barbeque. Aunt Inji was there and seeing her was the highlight of my week. Even though she was not the same happy outgoing person she was before the divorce, she still felt like home to me, my safe place.

The domestic violence she had endured and the subsequent divorce had noticeably chipped away at her bubbly self. The carefree, incredibly positive and outgoing person was now almost docile. It had affected her confidence and self-worth. From time to time, she would engage in "what if" conversations with Mother—What if she had stayed? What if she'd had children, or done things differently? Maybe she would still be married, maybe she could have made the relationship work.

I could see that she was now blaming herself for everything that happened, instead of seeing it for what it was—that she had been suffering under his abusive behaviour and nothing she had done would have made any difference. Aunt Inji had been in therapy for over a year and it seemed to be helping her cope, but she was still not back to her usual self. I suspected that this healing would take time.

I took a deep breath and held it in for a moment before releasing it again. I felt nothing but gratitude. The beautiful sky above me, sun gently making its presence and showering us with a touch of warmth on this lovely winter's day. I looked around me and acknowledged the people I cared about and the strength in them. Life had not been easy for any one of us, apart from Imran of course! He seemed to have always had it much easier than anyone else I know.

"How is my doctor in the making?" Aunt Inji said as she playfully nudged me on the shoulder.

"I am okay, just busy with life and uni," I replied with a long-stretched out smile.

"Remember if you have any questions or want help with assessments or projects you know I am happy to help in any way," Aunt Inji said tenderly.

I nodded back and said, "Yeah I know, I can always count on you."

If she only knew what kind of betrayal I was brewing behind her back at uni by befriending Humza! How disappointed would she be with me! I thought, feeling uncomfortable that I was not sharing something important with her.

But I was not friends with Humza, and it was more of an acquaintance if anything. And I was working hard towards ending that anyway. I was using avoidance as a strategy to try to make him get the drift—that I don't want to be around him. It's been an impossible mission so far, however, with Humza constantly hovering around me at every opportunity. If only he was not connected with Auntie Inji's ex-husband, then I would have happily welcomed his friendship.

"What about you? How is everything with you?" I asked as I took a sip of my green tea infused with cardamom.

"Well, you know—so, so. I am getting used to living by myself and I'm not as scared as I was when I initially moved into the apartment. It is weird living on my own. It's something I've never done before but I must admit that I'm starting to love my own company," Aunt Inji said as she giggled.

"The good news is that I'm sleeping a lot better now," Aunt Inji went on with a sense of relief in her voice.

"And I'm actually enjoying the process of getting

to know myself! Can't believe it has taken me so long to start my journey towards self-discovery! It must be a new world record at my age—I guess I'm a late bloomer!" she exclaimed as she let out an innocent laugh.

"I wish I had taken the time to really get to know who I am as a person before rushing into marrying a total stranger. I know that I had the choice to say no to the proposal but it felt like there was a chain around my ankles pulling me towards that predicted path," Aunt Inji said softly. "Like I needed to be married with kids before I was thirty. These shackles that society bind us women with—they're a heavy burden!" she continued as she looked down at the back of her hand, with a particular focus on her now bare wedding finger.

"The older I get, the more I'm realising the truth. The more I dislike being a woman. I mean look at Bilal, there is no set agenda for him and the direction of his life—he's living life like a free bird. It must be nice to live with that kind of privilege!" She turned her head to look at Uncle Bilal sitting there, talking and mucking around with Bahba.

I too turned around to look at Uncle Bilal, as Auntie Inji continued, "Sharing the same profession is not enough to marry someone. Okay, enough of me, I feel like I am babbling on and I'm probably not making any sense whatsoever! Sorry angel."

"You make perfect sense Aunt Inji," I managed to quickly say in reply.

"I too was just thinking that. I mean look at my brother Imran for example, he does little to nothing around the house, he barely lifts a finger and is adored by both Mother and Bahba. It is like he can do no wrong!" I said shaking my head disapprovingly.

"There's no pressure or timer on for when he is to marry. Almost like there is no space or capacity for misery in his life! Which don't get me wrong, I am so happy for him but why couldn't God give us women some of that shiny glitter in our lives too?" I said as I burst into laughter.

Aunt Inji joined in and laughed as she put her arm around me and gave me a gentle, affectionate squeeze.

"What are you crazy girls laughing about?" Grandmother asked as she slowly sat down next to us on the wooden garden seat.

Grandmother's legs were giving her grief. Her arthritis was playing up and her diabetes was also getting worst.

"Nothing really, just being silly," I said as

Grandmother delicately smiled at both me and Aunt Inji.

"You know, looking at you two I am so reminded of the young girls in our beautiful homeland in Kabul," Grandmother said as she now stared into space.

"My youngest sister Mariam and I used to have a large age gap like you two, but we were the closest amongst all the siblings. We just jelled together well," she said as she looked admiringly at both Aunt Inji and me.

"We used to run and hide under the grape vine arches in our backyard, just to evade the prospect of having to endure *Mullah* Ibrahim's torturous Quran lessons!" Grandmother let out a loud laugh, lifting her head backwards in pure, joyous nostalgia.

"Oh Grandmother, you were a bit of a rebel back in the day, weren't you?" I asked excitedly.

"Oh yes that I was. Us Afghan women are a lot stronger than the credit we are given," Grandmother said. "We go through a lot in our lives which starts at our Bahba's house growing up as a child, the sacrifices we make. Then 'sacrifice' becomes our middle name, which we carry with us as a wife, mother, and sister." She spoke now in a melancholy tone.

"This expectation to sacrifice our happiness, dreams and ourselves becomes the motto of our life without any actual consent from us, but more of an expectation," Grandmother continued as she took a deep breath, eyes heavy with moisture as she let out a sigh.

I gently touched the back of Grandmother's hand to comfort her.

Aunt Inji said, "Grandmother, perhaps it's strong Afghan women like us that need to do the hard work and be the foundation for real change—then we too, like the women in the West, can claim back our autonomy!"

"Things were remarkably similar if not identical here in the West not too many years ago Grandmother," Aunt Inji continued passionately. "These women had to fight for their rights; burn their bras in protest and so there is hope for us Afghan women too! One step at a time."

"You are so right my dear Injilla. We need to do the heavy lifting to make changes for not only women in our community but all women for generations to come. There is a saying that my Bahba, may he rest in peace, would use in a situation like this—'drop by drop will turn into a river,' he said." Grandmother took my hand in hers and gave it a gentle encouraging squeeze.

It was as if she had given us her blessings of approval.

Chapter 22

I ran across the hallway, thinking I was only five minutes late. Hopefully Mr Macalister wouldn't mind. Maybe he would be in a good mood for a change, and let this late entry slip by without any issues.

I slowly opened the door and snuck my head in to find the class buzzing and full of students, but no sign of Mr Macalister anywhere. That put a smile on my face as I entered the room and looked around for a place to sit. My eyes caught the only empty space in the tutorial room and I made my way towards it. Then a friendly hand waved frantically for me to hurry along, as if they had saved that spot especially for me, only to realise the hand belonged to none other than Humza! *How could this be happening again? Déjà vu!*

I made a sudden U-turn and headed back out the door. Taking a deep breath, I hovered in the doorway as my mind raced.

Here we go again! So awkward! How can I get out

of this situation? I thought.

I heard someone call my name. "Hey Zahra!" The voice came from the room I'd just left.

Not surprisingly, Humza was standing there waving and beckoning me to come in.

Suddenly I snapped. I turned around and headed over to him. Feeling frustrated, and without thinking, I muttered under my breath, "What is your problem? Leave me alone! Can't you take a hint? I don't want to have anything to do with you!"

Humza's face flushed pink and froze with his mouth half open.

"Hey, hey. I don't know what you mean. I just thought I was being kind by saving you a seat for Mr Macalister's lab tutorial," he said nervously.

"And why don't you want to have anything to do with me? What have I ever done to you?" he asked in protest.

"You are related to Uncle Omar, and I can't have anything to do with you at all! Do you have any clue what my Aunt Inji and my family has been through?" Without warning my eyes welled up, releasing their sorrow down my cheeks. I had now lost all control over my emotions.

"I am sorry, I didn't mean to upset you. But Zahra, I don't know what you are talking about," he said softly as he moved towards me.

"Uncle Omar is Aunt Inji's ex-husband! You were at their wedding where we first met and you said you were from the groom's side. So, you are related to him!" I exclaimed as I turned around and continue to walk away.

"Uncle Omar ... oh my goodness!" Humza said softly. "Hang on Zahra. I am not related to Omar. He is just a family friend of my parents that's all! I promise," Humza said convincingly as he walked close behind me.

"What? Do you mean you are not related to him?" I asked as I stopped walking and turned around to face him.

Humza's confused demeanour changed slowly to a slight smile as he said, "Exactly that! He is not family. His parents are family friends with my parents. I only see him on special occasions like Eid or weddings but apart from that I barely know him."

I felt my cheeks getting warmer and warmer. The realisation that I had just behaved like a mad woman had started to sink in. What made it worst was that Humza's smile started to turn into a giggle and then a loud laugh as I quickly wiped my tears, now overwhelmed with sheer embarrassment!

"Well do you two need a second invite to attend

class or are you going in? Seeing you both are already ten minutes late?" asked a sarcastic voice from behind us. It was Mr Macalister.

We both promptly went back into the classroom without another word. As Humza sat down next to me, I sank into the seat as if I was made of wax and gradually melted into place. As I was unpacking, I snuck in a quick glance at Humza, and he was smiling and still giggling about what happened earlier.

He must think I am nuts!

I felt so embarrassed. It was such an awkward situation to say the least, so how would I ever look at him in the eyes again or even talk to him?

Mr Macalister's voice droned on in the background as I kept replaying the earlier scenario in my head.

Humza's smile seemed to be getting deeper each time I sneaked a glance at his face. *Such a mesmerising smile as well, as I have noticed before.*

I felt myself melting even more, not over what had just happened but what I was seeing—his pearly white teeth and the most chiselled looking dimples I have ever seen! I thought to myself, *He is enjoying himself a little too much over this whole thing.*

I couldn't help but smile back. Although so

embarrassing, the whole situation had become very funny. I felt a sense of relief that I was not betraying Aunt Inji after all. Slowly, a sense of calm came over me. *This means that I don't have to avoid or ignore Humza anymore! I can be around him,* I thought. *But I'm still not sure if this is a good thing or not.*

I took out my post-it notes and wrote "I AM SORRY" accompanied by a smiley face and pushed the pad towards him as a signal that he should respond.

Humza picked up the note, smiled at me and then wrote something and pushed the notepad back in front of me. It read, "Nice try but you're not getting off the hook this easily!"

I looked at him and smiled as I nodded in agreement. I had behaved so badly that I would happily take any punishment that he dished out. It was such a relief to know that Humza was not related to Uncle Omar and that I was not betraying my family by associating with him.

"Lunch with me, today! I won't take no for an answer this time," the post-it note from Humza read.

I smiled at him expressing my consent to the invitation. I felt a flutter of emotions float around in my stomach, the positive kind.

I didn't know what it was about Humza and why he had this effect on me, but whatever it was, I liked how I felt when I was around him.

Chapter 23

The past eight months of uni seemed to have passed so quickly. As the spring weather was kicking in, the flowers were blooming and the sun was noticeably honouring the sky with its presence more often! My favourite time of year was springtime.

My life was finally settling down and I had some good things happening. Uni was one of them and the other was my family.

It seemed that Mother might have finally let bygones be bygones with what happened with, you know, "It." I tried not to think about what happened to me as a child because if I opened that door to the past, I would find myself debilitated in so many ways—physically, emotionally, and mentally—for days and sometimes weeks at a time. I had learnt that if I acknowledged what happened but did not dwell on it, if I did not revisit those traumatic memories in detail, it would help me in my journey toward healing.

I refused to let what happened to me define me

as a person. I would not let this be a life sentence. I acknowledged it happened, it was awful and what I endured after that was even worse and, to some extent, I still suffered from it. But I had learnt to accept that it was not my fault. Really, I had. I had been just an innocent child. I refused to let it pave my path in life and haunt me into my future!

It had taken me a long time, but I had learnt to forgive myself and I was focusing on strengthening and repairing my relationship with Mother. I needed to let go of all that anger, some of which I still held inside—about how she treated me like a *faisha*; how she failed to protect me; and how she failed to stand up for me or support me.

Mother had simply pretended it hadn't happened and she had punished me throughout my childhood. I guess she was trying to make sure that I turned out to be a good person.

But she had treated "It" like he had not done anything wrong or as if nothing had even happened—complete denial! I still didn't understand the logic behind that.

"Okay are you going to keep staring out the window or will you actually wash the dishes too?" Mother smiled at me and gently tapped me on the back of the head.

I smiled back, unsure why Mother was in such a rush today. It was Sunday and she had been fussing over the appearance of the house all day.

"I didn't think the family were coming today, Mother. Is Auntie Inji coming or are we expecting a guest?" I asked curiously.

Mother looked up at me with a mischievous smile and said, "Not Auntie Inji but there is a special guest coming."

My curiosity deepened. "Who is this special guest Mother?"

"Well, you know there comes a time in every girl's life when they need to go on their own journey and start their own life," Mother said with an excited wide smile on her face.

Why am I not liking the vibe Mother is giving me right at this moment?

"What does that mean Mother?" I asked, half suspecting what she was referring to but hoping that it was just my imagination going wild!

"You know that you are not a child anymore Zahra. You've graduated from school and you're at university now, so it is time to start thinking about your future," she said in a soft yet excited tone.

My heart plunged like I was on one of those rides in a Wonderland theme park but without a secure harness or belt for protection! Is Mother suggesting what I think she is suggesting? My mind was racing and I felt a sense of foreboding. *This is not good!*

"Yes, I am paving my way toward my career and future, Mother, and I'm going to uni to help achieve this," I replied in an innocent yet direct tone.

"Of course, silly! What I mean is in terms of a life partner and having your own family. In case you haven't noticed you are not a little girl anymore!" Mother said conspiratorially.

Then her voice changed to a light-hearted tone. "Later tonight we have a nice young man coming to ask for your hand in marriage."

A rush of anger and shock came over me. After everything we had been through with Auntie Inji and Uncle Omar, how Mother could even be thinking of marriage and arranging me was beyond belief!

"Mother you didn't think to tell me or ask me how I feel about this?" I asked defensively.

"I am telling you now, aren't I?" Mother said with a sudden change in her tone.

"Mother I am not a child! Please stop treating me like one!" I was showing my annoyance now and was daring a slightly angry tone.

Mothers' eyebrows arched. "Yes, you're an adult now! You're eighteen! No matter how long we live in Australia, we have our own culture and traditions that we follow. Your age doesn't mean shit to me. Do you understand?"

I felt the storm brewing and heading straight towards me, ready to shake my world to the core once again. *I'm not sure if I have the patience to take on another battle with Mother so soon.* I was raging inside as I tried to get some control over the conversation before it turned into World War 3. But I wondered if it was too late—had the battle already started?

"Of course, Mother. But having a voice about my future doesn't make me Australian, it just makes me human!" I said sternly.

I saw Mother's face transform from being unhappy to totally distorted with rage.

Now I need to prepare myself for the aftermath. I am asking for it aren't I? I thought. *But what choice do I have? This time I must stand up for myself.*

"*Marggh*! Leave the kitchen at once before I lose it! And wear something decent and do your hair! We don't want him to get a glimpse of you and get frightened off!" Mother exclaimed in utter fury.

I quickly made my way out of the kitchen to avoid more conflict with her. I was coming to realise that Mother still had control over me. I still feared her and felt like a lost and abandoned child who craved love and attention.

I entered my bedroom and slammed the door shut behind me I was angry and harbouring such strong emotions.

What is happening to me now? Can't I catch a break from this horrible life of mine? Just when I am starting to enjoy life at home with Mother; just when I am getting a sense of what it is like to be happy and at peace and to have dreams and hopes, this is thrown at me.

Chapter 24

The sky was draped in the most beautiful light pink, baby blue and burnt orange as the sun made its way down behind the hills. I lay on the ground for a moment enjoying the stunning spectacle above. The Sydney sky during sunset reminded me of fairy floss with its beautiful baby pink and blue shades taking over. Such beautiful fuel for the soul! I was relaxing in the university grounds, lying on soft grass with my head cushioned by my backpack.

"Here you are, lazy bones! I looked everywhere for you. We'd better get going or we'll miss the beginning of the lecture," Humza said enthusiastically.

I raised my head and saw Humza's face.

"Hey. Oh no! I don't want to be late again," I said. "I'm always lost in my own world. Come on let's go!" I quickly rummaged around, packing my belongings.

"Hahaha! I am joking Miss Gullible! We have another half an hour to go before class starts. You are so easy to trick," Humza clapped his hands and kept laughing, so pleased with himself.

I felt annoyed that I was such an easy target for him, and he had successfully fooled me yet again!

"Ha, ha, very funny Humza. I'm glad you're happy you got me," I said, feeling slightly irritated.

Humza playfully nudged me on the shoulder. "Why the long face? I was just mucking around with you."

"Nothing, I am okay," I managed to say.

Humza and I had become close friends over the past months, but I wasn't sure if I could tell him about what happened on the weekend with Mother and her Mister Perfect Mustafa the suitor!

"Come on, I can see there is something brewing inside those beautiful beady eyes of yours," Humza said. "You never know, I might be able to help. I am not completely useless you know," a cheeky smile showing off his pearly whites.

"Hey, my eyes are not beady!" I said as I playfully pushed him on the shoulder. "And I don't know. To be honest, I don't think you would understand or even get where I'm coming from," I managed to say without giving away too much.

"Give me a go, for goodness sake! If we are not on the same page, then you can end the conversation right there and then. No questions asked," he said in a more sensible tone.

"Okay, no laughing or carrying on. If you disagree, say it and it ends there. I am not having a debate about it. I can't handle another person on the list of those telling me that I'm wrong!" I said setting clear boundaries about my limits.

"Agreed," Humza exclaimed without hesitation.

I really hoped Humza would take me seriously, as I couldn't keep this to myself for much longer. If Auntie Inji hadn't been at the medical conference in Melbourne for the week then I would have spoken with her, but I didn't want to call her there and bother her over the phone.

"Well on the weekend something happened at my house that I was totally unprepared for. I was completely taken off guard. So Mother was running around and cleaning the house frantically and I assumed that she had some guests coming over and so I asked her. Mother said, 'I have a suitor coming over to see you, to see if HE likes you'!" I said with distaste.

"Oh okay. So let me see if I have this right. So, you had no heads up from your mum about this?" Humza asked with a confused expression on his face.

"No, Mother didn't feel the need to tell me

beforehand or talk about the matter before inviting him and his family over," I replied, annoyed.

"Well okay, I get why you are upset about this," Humza said supportively.

"But the solution is simple. Speak with your mum about how you feel and what you want in life. Ask your mum to talk to you and discuss the proposal, before she organises for a suitor to come over to meet you," he said wisely.

"I wish it was that simple Humza," I managed to say. Obviously, he hadn't met Mother so he didn't know what she was like!

"So, what happened? Did it go okay?" he asked in an inquisitive tone.

"It was awful! I felt like I was in a shop front window on show like I was being displayed for HIM to see if I tick all HIS boxes so he can marry me! I felt embarrassed and I never want to go through that ever again," I said looking down at the ground in shame.

I hadn't been able to talk to anyone about this, I mean really talk, but I was definitely comfortable speaking with Humza.

"I am sorry Zahra. I honestly can't imagine how uncomfortable that would have felt," Humza said sympathetically.

He gets it! I was in shock. *I thought he would have no idea—because he is a guy after all and guys get to do the window shopping; and they aren't the items on display! For him to sympathise with me, I mean to really understand that it was such a difficult experience for me is a breath of fresh air!*

As he lifted his face to look at me with eyes full of empathy, I thought, *I wish someone in my family looked at me with the same emotional connection and understanding about all this. Am I asking for too much?*

I suddenly caught myself staring at him for far too long!

"Thank you for understanding," I stammered, embarrassed. "I honestly thought you would have no clue being a … guy and all," I quickly snatched my gaze away from those captivating brown eyes before I could become spellbound again.

Humza chuckled slightly and said, "A bit of a news flash for you Zahra. Yes, that part is true, I am a guy, but I am not made of stone and I do have a heart in this buff perfect chest of mine. I don't know what type of guys you've been around, but I am not like that — 'Pretty Eyes'!" he said cheekily.

Could he be any more perfect? I thought as I managed to work on a smile in reply. I felt tears prickling behind my eyes as they threatened to overflow. But I made sure it didn't happen. *I don't want Humza to think I am weak and that I cry at the drop of a hat!*

I loved it when he called me "Pretty Eyes"! I had noticed that it had become his nickname for me and he'd been using it often lately. This, and also "beady eyes" which makes me laugh.

Humza reached out and gently touched my shoulder. "I am sorry. I didn't mean to make you upset."

I tried to regain my composure. "No please don't apologise, you haven't done anything wrong. I appreciate your words of support. It means a lot to me, coming from you."

It felt weird that this guy, who I hadn't known for very long at all, could feel my pain and listen to me with more empathy than my own Mother and Bahba. At least I have Imran and now Humza on my team—they could both see where I was coming from. I was sure Aunt Inji would also understand and agree with me once I told her. But must admit I was totally taken off guard by Humza's response. *He actually understands my opinion on the medieval ritual of arranged marriages.*

I could feel the warmth of his hand on my shoulder more intensely, comforting me. It felt nice to have the kindness of another human expressed in such humble and pure way.

"To show emotion is to be human and we feel things! It is not weird at all. Anyway, you didn't tell me the ending of what happened on the weekend. As in what happened to the poor suitor. Did he meet the criteria or was he a total failure?" Humza lightened the mood with his cheeky tone.

I smiled and said, "Well he seemed like a nice enough guy. He is a pharmacist and looked okay and seemed like a good person when he spoke to me. But that's not the point. After everything that Aunt Inji went through and suffered haven't they learnt anything?"

"I don't believe in arranging two complete strangers to marry. I also don't believe in dating every guy or girl one meets. All I am saying is, let them speak on several occasions, meet outside the family setting without multiple eyes glaring and judging them to see if they are truly compatible," I said with conviction.

"Everyone, listen to 'Zahra the match maker'! She knows what she's talking about and will help find you your soul mate," Humza said amusingly at the top of his lungs as he stood up.

I couldn't help myself but laugh and be entertained by Humza yet once again.

Chapter 25

I am driving my car. Driving makes me feel like I am flying! Once I get into my little silver Toyota Corolla nothing can hold me back. I am as free as a bird!

"Why do you always have your head in the clouds like some possessed gypsy girl?" Imran asked, breaking into my little bubble of happy thoughts.

"What are you on about?" I chuckled, knowing exactly what he meant.

"You'll have to come down to earth and deal with the situation eventually, Zahra! And you know Mother always gets her way," Imran said with a cheeky smile.

I was glad to have Imran in my life. He provided that balance between those of my family who are always giving those stressful and anxious vibes and the bubbly yet caring vibe that Imran brings into the mix. We may no longer be innocent children, but Imran still has that carefree, happy go lucky attitude about life! I loved this about him and prayed that he would stay this way, that life wouldn't change him.

"Yes, I know and I'm working on Mother. It just takes time, that's all." I said this without feeling convinced myself. I really didn't know if I'd be able to change Mother's mind.

"So, what's the plan? Are you thinking of running away, and if so, can I come with you?" Imran asked in a comical voice with a huge Luna Park-like smile on his face.

"Of course not! What are you deranged or something? Why would I run away?" I was slightly irritated by his suggestion, and the fact that he is not taking this seriously.

"Are you serious? Have you not realised that with Mother it is either her way or the highway, nothing in between?" Imran said, serious this time.

I looked down and reached for the hand brake, lifting it up, and brought the car to a complete stop. "Look, Imran," I said with determination. "I don't want this to turn into a battle between me and Mother but I am not laying down for this one. Every other time I've been at odds with her I have declared defeat immediately without putting up a fight or having my opinion heard. That is not me, that is not Zahra anymore!"

In response, Imran placed his hand on my shoulder as I was about to get out of the car, wanting my complete attention.

"Zahra, I stand with you, and I will be here to support you," he said with commitment. "I agree with you on this. You should get the right to decide or at least have a say in who you marry. It is a lifelong commitment—particularly with what happened with Aunty Inji—and I don't want history to repeat itself," Imran said kindly.

Law school has been really good for Imran, I thought. I can hear his ability to relate and put himself in someone else's shoes. The maturity is finally showing up. A little late, no doubt, but it's good to see it developing finally! It's a proud young sister moment for me for sure.

I leaned forward and hugged Imran tightly. I desperately needed to hear this even though Mother would see Imran's support as me manipulating Imran and getting into his head. This gave me the strength that I needed to stand up to Mother. Bahba has rarely stood up for himself, so I was not expecting him to do anything in my favour. He usually went along with whatever Mother said.

"Thank you, Imran, for being you! I needed this. Someone from my own family who stands up for my basic right as a human being," I said, emotion creeping into my voice.

Careful Zahra, I thought. *You need to keep it*

together for when you go home and face Mother.

As we entered the house, Grandmother's beautiful face lit up the room, sitting there in her delicate, see-through white scarf. *Such a beautiful surprise! I haven't seen Grandmother in weeks.* I ran and kissed Grandmother's hand as a mark of respect and gave her a long overdue hug.

"Here is the beautiful girl we were just talking about," Grandmother said with a lovely soothing smile.

"How are you Grandmother? It feels like I haven't seen you for so long!" I said as I hugged her again.

"Hi Mother," I said as I went to put my uni bag in my room.

"Hi. Quick, go get ready as the suitor and his family are coming over later this evening for one more time before we move forward with the next step in the process," Mother said with a tone of great importance.

My heart sank. *What is she on about with "move forward to the next step in the process?"*

Imran sat down and the expression on Grandmother's face was evident that a storm was brewing in the living room. And it was about to hit full blast at any moment!

"Mother I am not going to see him or anyone else for that matter. I am completing my studies and that is all I want to focus on for now," I replied in a gentle yet firm tone.

"Well, it is a good thing no one asked you for your opinion about the matter. Zahra I am not asking you. I am telling you. Go and put on the dress that I have laid on your bed and get ready. Everyone, including your Aunt Inji, will be here soon," she said loudly, trying to keep her anger under control.

My heart started beating like a drum! *How could Mother do this to me, invite everyone here, yet again, behind my back and without my knowledge!*

I turned to face her directly as I exclaimed, "I am not going to wear any dress! There are not going to be any suitors coming to see me."

With rage in my heart and anger in my eyes I continued, "I am not a piece of furniture or clothing that you can give away! I know you don't see me, but I am human!"

Mother's face turned scarlet as she started with her barrage of abuse, "You *faisha*! You will never change. You will ruin this family, and our name will be dishonoured yet again! You will get in that room and get ready or so help me God!"

"You can call me all the names under the sun, but I am not getting ready or marrying anyone! Do what you like to me," I said with sheer fury.

"I am not afraid! There is nothing left that you could possibly do or say to me, Mother, to hurt me—you've managed to do it all," I said as tears barraged down my face.

I looked at my grandmother. Her distressed face was breaking my heart. I didn't want things to go down like this. I wanted a civil conversation to convince Mother against this arranged marriage mess! But Mother had to do it her way. And she did it by using coercive control and manipulation.

Well Mother's guilt trip is not going to get her what she wants this time!

Suddenly Imran stood up and said, "Mother at least listen to her. Let's sit down and have a calm conversation and hear her out."

Mother threw the metal pot in her hand in my direction, narrowly missing me. She pushed past Imran, shoving him in the chest to get to me. Imran landed on the floor as Mother grabbed me by the hair and aggressively jerked my head from side to side.

Needles of pain seared through my scalp, but the pain in my heart was worse.

I could hear Grandmother's voice, "Leave her alone! Have you gone mad?"

I managed to release myself from Mother's grip and ran into my bedroom slamming the door behind me. I dived into bed and cried. I wished I was dead.

I could hear the clamour of raised voices between Grandmother, Imran and Mother. I could not make out what they were saying, but there was screaming back and forth between them.

It was an awful feeling to know that I was the cause of all that! I didn't know if I was doing the right thing, but I was not ready for marriage and letting a stranger get close to me! Maybe there was something wrong with me?

I could barely make out what Mother was saying but I did hear this, "Okay well if she is going to live under my roof and not abide by my rules then she can say goodbye to university. She's trying to make me look like I am the bad person, but I will really show her what bad looks like!"

My heart felt like it was diving in an ocean so deep and so dark! Uni was my little ray of light. It gave me hope for the future. It made me believe that I would do some good in this world. How could Mother punish me like this and try to take that away from me!

I could hear Mother on the phone in the background. "Yes she's come home from uni with a very bad cough and we wouldn't want that to spread and for you all to fall ill too."

I suspected that she was speaking with the suitor's family and cancelling tonight's event.

Thank God for that! I thought. *At least this buys me some time to convince Mother against this circus.*

A few minutes after that I could hear crying in a distant part of the house. It was Mother. "That girl will be the end of me, you watch," I heard her say.

Chapter 26

I heard a soft voice gently say, "Wake up princess, it's nearly noon." I opened my eyes and there was Aunty Inji sitting on the side of my bed, running her hand gently through my hair.

What a beautiful sight to wake up to! I thought.

Seeing Aunty Inji gave me hope that everything would be okay. She was like a lantern for me, illuminating my path in life with a bright light. I wondered if she knew the latest about my ban from uni by Mother in retaliation for not agreeing to see the suitor last night.

"Hi. When did you come over?" I asked as I rubbed my eyes. I was struggling to focus on Aunty Inji's silhouette.

"My flight was delayed so I got here quite late last night. It sounds like I missed the blow up," she said softly with an encouraging smile.

I lifted myself up and sat up leaning against the bedhead. I felt like such a disappointment to myself, to my family and to my community.

Why is it such a heavy burden to speak up and to have an opinion about my own life? I thought as Aunty Inji held me in her sympathetic gaze.

"Yes, you missed a lot! You missed me causing my family pain and hurt. But what's new, right?" I chuckled sarcastically with rush of emotions swelling up in my throat. I lowered my head in shame, pretending to fix my sleeve.

"No lovely, don't say that. You haven't done anything wrong. You're just trying to have a say about your future and there's nothing wrong with that!" Aunty Inji lifted my chin with her hand to raise my gaze to hers.

Is this a dream or does Aunt Inji actually agree with me?

"What?" I asked abruptly.

"Yes, marriage is not a joke! Look at me and the mess my life has become. Don't rush into anything without really knowing what you are getting into. That's my advice!" Aunt Inji said gently in a supportive tone.

"I wish I'd had this much courage to stand up for myself and say no to Omar. I had a gut feeling about him early on. All the signs were there but I felt it was too late to back out. 'What would everyone say,' I thought," Aunt Inji said as she turned her head to look out the window, her eyes full of sorrow.

I felt a sense of relief on hearing this. And feeling validated was nice. I was starting to feel as if I'd made the right decision—to stand up for myself and have a voice about my future and have a say about who I spent the rest of my life with.

I grabbed Aunt Inji with both hands and hugged her tight. I needed this and wanted it from Mother so badly, even though, deep down, I knew that it could never happen.

I don't know why I don't learn! I thought.

I kept hoping for the impossible when it came to Mother. I guess this is the essence of a relationship between a parent and child. Always wanting to be accepted and loved no matter how many times one was disappointed and sent away empty handed.

"Aww luv. I am sorry that we were born into a family where this has to be such a battle," Aunty Inji said in a sincere tone as she hugged me back tightly.

"It makes me feel like I am the worst person ever, when I try talk to Mother about this. The self-doubt creeps in and takes over," I said as I let go of Aunt Inji's embrace.

"But deep down, deep within my own thoughts, I know that I am not wrong in how I feel about this whole thing. It is so frustrating because I see this could be a massive mistake, yet Mother and Bahba are so lost in the entire process and ceremonial aspect of the practice that they seem to have no space to give my feelings any thought." I leaned back, resting on the bedhead.

"Sadly, I can relate!" Aunt Inji said as she looked down at her bare wedding ring finger where a wedding band once sat. "In hindsight the situation with Omar might have been avoided if I had really got to know him before diving into marriage. I honestly believe if I'd had some more time with him, and got to know him to see if we were compatible, we both could have avoided the heartbreak and misery," she continued.

"We all deserve to be happy—to find the right person for us to share our lives with. In all this, the one criticism I have is this idea of not wanting to ever marry. You too, my sunshine, deserve to be happy. You deserve to have someone to love and care for you and to care for them too!" Aunt Inji said as she looked deep into my eyes to see my reaction.

For me to be loved—what would that be like? I wondered. *For one person in this massive world to put me first and to love me unconditionally! I can't imagine that right at this moment or even how much joy it has the potential of bringing.*

"The worst part of all this is that Mother said she will not let me continue with my studies if I don't agree with the wedding proposal. She knows how super important that is to me. How could she do this to me, knowing how hard I've worked to get to where I am?" I felt so frustrated, trying to make sense of it as my emotions eased up and I could feel some calmness come over me.

"Leave that to me," Aunt Inji said as she stood up and started to pace back and forth.

"I will speak with your mother. I know how to get through to her gently. If you speak with her, it will just make her angrier, because she sees you as being a defiant child," Aunt Inji said as she turned to face me.

"You are her child, and she will always feel that need for you to obey her and for her to have the last word. But with me it is an even playing field. And my words will have a different weight, coming from another adult—not to mention a doctor!" Aunt Inji said as she smirked slightly, taking advantage of her respected status as a medical practitioner. Her comment made me snicker a little.

I felt such a relief that I wouldn't have to endure this burden on my own. I desperately hoped that

Aunt Inji could get through to Mother. She could be very stubborn when she wanted to be. The only good thing in my life was going to uni and if that was no longer there then I would literally lose my mind!

"Angel, stop this overthinking! Everything will be okay, I promise. Quickly get dressed. Your mother just stepped out to get groceries. That will give us just enough time to escape and get some fresh air by the beach side," she said in an almost schoolgirl like tone. Like we were about to break all the rules without a care!

I quickly got up and out of bed and headed to the bathroom to wash up.

* * *

Sitting next to Aunt Inji in the car, I realised it had been so long since we had last gone out together. With her hectic doctor's schedule and my crazy Med school timetable, our paths rarely crossed.

I smiled at her, hopeful but not convinced that she would succeed in convincing Mother.

"By the way of curiosity, is the suitor nice looking? Is he worth investing some time with, to get to know him better?" Aunt Inji said with a cheeky smile smeared across her face. "You never know, after all!"

"What?" I responded in shock.

"Look, I'm not saying you must marry the guy but, like, can you see a future with him? Do you get butterflies in your stomach or feel some sort of chemistry?" Aunt Inji was being inquisitive! Her cheeky, old, bubbly personality seemed to be slowly returning, which was wonderful!

"No! I don't know what you are on about with the butterflies!" I replied innocently. But deep down I felt those butterflies in the pit of my stomach, but not for the suitor or anyone else except for when I was around Humza. I had not given it much thought or realised it till today.

When I was around Humza I felt like I was floating high in the clouds. The butterflies came and went, particularly the other day when we were talking about the suitor situation, and he was comforting me. His touch had sent me on an emotional rainbow roller coaster with multiple shades of butterflies. I had never felt this way with anyone before and I was not sure of this foreign feeling. But it was very pleasant!

"By the way, what does it mean to get butterflies, Aunt Inji?" I inquisitively asked. I wanted to understand this new feeling.

"Well, that's one sign that you are in love with

the person who's giving you such a nice high feeling! This should have been a sign for me with Omar. I never felt this rush of emotions and butterflies with him at all!" Aunt Inji said disappointedly as she drove, looking straight ahead at the road that lay before us.

"I'd just assumed that I needed to give it time for that to happen—time for that rush of emotions to erupt like a volcano!

"But looking back, there was one person who gave me those emotions back during my uni days. I felt so confused back then, not knowing what to make of it," Aunt Inji said in pure nostalgia.

"What do you mean Aunt Inji? You never mentioned this before!" I was intrigued by this news.

"Because I simply didn't understand the feelings, nor could I make sense of it myself at the time. Our culture is such that we are taught to suffocate such feelings of euphoria and see them as lust or pure sin! Especially if you are a female," Aunt Inji said with a wave of sadness in her eyes.

I rested my hand gently on her shoulder. Aunt Inji turned to look at me and smiled.

"I was in my second year of Med school and Shahbaz was in all my core unit lectures and tutorials. He was a Muslim Pakistani, born in

Sydney with immigrant parents," Aunt Inji said as she went deeper into her nostalgic trance.

"What was he like Aunt Inji?" I asked impatiently, interrupting her.

"He was tall with dark features. Long lashes that went on for days and he had a very captivating smile!" she replied.

"More than that he was kind and gentle. Not like other men I knew. It was like he had all the good features of a good Afghan or Muslim man with an infusion of the western chivalry and an extra dollop of intelligence!" Aunt Inji giggled like a schoolgirl.

"Well, I am now confused! Are you describing a person or did we change the subject and are we now talking about a dessert?" I laughed hysterically, raising my hand up to cover my mouth.

Now Aunt Inji was also laughing uncontrollably. "I promise you one thing, my dear Zahra, we will be the force towards change, and we will break this cycle of patriarchy and sacrifice! I don't mean that we go rogue. I mean we can operate within the realm of our religion, but not to the point that our rights are drowned! We cannot be forced to blindly enter arrangements that are seen in our community as the 'right' thing to do," Aunt Inji said passionately.

Chapter 27

Returning to uni after two weeks felt strange. It was like being a new kid starting school again. I was looking around nervously trying to familiarise myself and reclaim my territory. It felt good to be back though. It was where I most wanted to be and where I felt the most comfortable.

I looked up at the sky, taking a deep breath through my nose and holding it for a few seconds before releasing the rush of air out through my mouth. Along with that release went the heavy feeling on my shoulders that had burdened my body with stress.

To say I was shocked that Mother had changed her mind by allowing me to return to uni would be an understatement! I honestly thought this was going to be it for me—I would be stuck at home with Mother, cooking and cleaning all day long. Aunt Inji's persuasion skills must have been really impressive!

I knew for sure that Mother was not happy about

going back on her threat to take away my rights to attend uni, and in my heart I commended her for seeing the situation for what it was—that this was an opportunity for me to have a bright future and taking it away would benefit no one.

I excitedly walked towards our usual seating area—there was a magnificent gum tree, with leaves cascading down, creating a veil from the sun and offering cool patches of shade for us all to sit under. Its dried leaves crunched beneath my sneakers. I took a moment to appreciate the natural beauty around me.

I felt a thrill of happiness that I would be seeing my friends again, and most of all Humza, after so long. I was yet to tell him why I hadn't been at uni all this time. As I lifted my head, I saw the usual crew with the girls and Humza seated on the bench. But to my shock, Angela was seated on his lap and Mina was leaning on his back. I watched as he pushed Angela off his lap and reached for his bag—it seemed as if he was searching for something in it.

As I took the next step, I froze, shocked by what I had just witnessed.

I knew he was incredibly attractive and so dreamy but why was he letting the girls drape all over him like that? I felt horrified by what I had seen.

It doesn't look like he has missed me at all! I thought, feeling devastated. *Maybe I mean nothing to Humza after all. Is it all in my imagination that we have become good friends? Maybe the truth is that I'm just another bimbo added to his list of admirers.*

A wave of heartbreak took hold of me. I began to feel a sharp, stabbing pain in my chest. These girls always sat with us in a group under the shade of the gum tree, but I had never seen them touching Humza like that before. *Why am I so affected by what I've just witnessed?* I turned and slowly walked in the opposite direction, away from the group.

"Hey stranger, where have you been?" I heard a voice from behind me as I continued to walk away without looking back. But I recognised the voice as Humza's as I increased my pace.

"Oi you, didn't you hear me call out to you?" he asked as he tapped me gently on the shoulder.

I turned around feeling hurt and now angry with Humza as I suddenly blurted out without thinking, "Don't you dare touch me! I am not like those other girls who are all over you like leeches!"

I didn't understand my own reaction, but such responses seemed to be happening more often with me these days. Of course, my behaviour towards Humza was completely irrational — he hadn't done anything wrong with regards to me at all!

"Hey, hey. Calm down, what has got into you? You turn up after so long and in such a foul mood?" Humza said softly with his hands in front of his chest like he was surrendering to me.

"Nothing, just leave me alone!" I managed to say as I continued to walk away from him.

He jogged alongside me and said, "Come on let's sit somewhere and talk about this. Is everything okay at home?"

"You have Angela to keep you busy, so go talk to her!" I said in a pure tone of malice. I was aware of the immaturity of my behaviour, yet I couldn't seem to stop it.

"Hang on, hang on a minute. Are you jealous of Angela and Mina?" he asked with a sense of epiphany and humour in his voice.

Oh no, I think he's right! Why else would I have a reaction to Humza having fun with other girls? It must be related to the feeling I get in my gut—the butterflies and heart racing—when I'm alone with him.

Having made this realisation I really needed to get a grip and bring my emotions under control, otherwise my silence would make his accusation of being jealous seem true!

Humza was now laughing uncontrollably as he

strode along next to me, trying to keep up.

"Oh my god, you are! Well, I don't know what to say, but I take this as a compliment," Humza said as he snickered.

"Seems to me you care about me like I do about you. In fact, I care a lot about you Zahra!" he announced.

"I have missed you so much these two weeks. I think you missed the part where I tried to push Angela off me. It makes me feel uncomfortable when girls think it's okay for them to behave like that towards me just because I am a guy," he blurted out in the heat of the moment.

What is he trying to say? I wondered while still angrily striding toward the cafeteria.

"Stop for a minute Zahra, please!" he said as he gently took hold of my wrist.

I stopped and stood there, feeling paralysed by his gentle touch. Slowly the anger started to transform into a whirlwind of butterflies, with my heart racing and my knees weakening.

"Listen to me for a minute and then you can walk away or do whatever you want! Sit with me for a moment and give me a chance to explain myself," he pleaded in a gentle tone. He guided me towards the outdoor seating area near the cafeteria.

I was glad to sit down as my legs were getting wobbly to the point where I was finding it hard to continue to stand or walk.

He looked deep into my eyes as he continued. "You know, some girls can be very dominating, for want of a better word. I've told Angela many times I am not comfortable with her behaviour but it doesn't seem to make any difference. They're my friends, yes, but not that special person in my life that everyone dreams of."

I thought my heart would jump right out of my chest and sit on the table, it was beating so fast and so hard as I listened to Humza speak!

"I don't know why I feel this way about you, but I know one thing. I have never felt this way about anyone before," he said.

"Zahra, I feel like I have a crazy strong connection with you and I can be myself when I'm around you. I admire your morals, ethics and dedication to your family and your studies. You are beautiful, kind and intelligent!" he said sincerely as his cheeks started to blush.

"I don't want to lose your friendship, and I know by saying this I will risk losing you all together but if I don't say anything and lose you, I will be devastated. Your friendship means the world to me, and I have grown to really like you. I want to be with you now and into the future," he said as he gently reached out for my hand and held it in his.

"Zahra, I want to spend the rest of my life with you and marry you. I love you, Pretty Eyes," he said with my hand still in his.

I was frozen like I had been dipped in snow. I couldn't move a muscle or my tongue. I honestly didn't see this coming! I mean I knew we got along well and were of a similar mind and passionate about medicine, but for Humza to love me and want to marry me—this was totally unexpected. Especially when Mother had always said, "Who in their right mind would want to marry you!"

My eyes welled up with tears, like a river ready to burst its bank. No one had ever said such wonderful things about me let alone all at thc same time! It felt so strange hearing those things about myself, especially from a boy, and a boy I liked!

Before I could muster up the courage to say anything he continued, "That is if you feel the same way and want to be with me and marry me of course!"

That's classic Humza, gentle and thoughtful. But I can't believe he feels the same way about me! He likes me and wants to marry me!

Chapter 28

After a few moments of silence, I finally gathered the strength to say, "Humza, you are an amazing guy. You have all the qualities that any girl would want in a guy. You are kind, considered and highly intelligent."

"Phew, at least you didn't have ugly as part of that list!" Humza said nervously trying to crack a joke to lighten up the serious mood.

I giggled slightly and snorted to my surprise. In return Humza laughed and asked, "But jokes aside, do you at least feel the same way or have any feelings for me?"

I was fidgeting with the tissue in my hand, that Humza had thoughtfully got for me earlier as I was getting teary. I was so nervous, not knowing what to say.

What should I say to him? In the back of my mind, I could hear Mother's voice and what she would think and say about this.

Without further thought the words tumbled

out of my mouth without warning, "I do really like you Humza. I never thought I would feel the way I feel about you towards any guy!"

"I don't exactly know what love is, if that's what you are asking, but when I am around you, I am happy. I get excited just at the thought of seeing you at uni. You make me feel special and I like being in your company," I managed to say as I noticed Humza's facial expression change from anxious to relieved.

I knew I was about to burst the happy bubble. "But I am not the right person for you. You deserve better," I said quickly.

"No, no Zahra I love you and can't live without you!" he blurted out, then paused holding his breath, with worry on his face. He must have been second guessing himself on whether he was being too pushy or needy.

I couldn't help but smile at him as he flirtatiously reciprocated the smile.

"Sorry I didn't mean to be so blunt but now my true feelings are out. That is how I feel and what is this nonsense about you not being the right person for me? You are perfect!" Humza said whole heartedly.

As much as I was over the moon about this

revelation from Humza, I had so much on my plate with the suitor situation. I couldn't even contemplate how all this would go down with Mother!

"Thank you for being honest and telling me how you feel about me. It means so much to me. No one has ever said such lovely things to me before, especially a guy," I said as I looked up to meet his eyes in a united gaze.

"But Humza, my life at the moment is very complicated. With the whole suitor situation there is no room for this, as much as I want it," I said in an emotional tone as I lowered my head to look at the now moist tissue Humza had given me earlier.

Humza reached out and gently touched the back of my hand.

"I hear what you are saying Zahra, but I am happy to wait for you as long as it takes. So long as you don't make me wait till I am old and grey!" he said as his face switched from serious face to a slightly playful smile.

I was basking in this feeling of being loved the way the dry Sydney sun evaporates the occasional surprise rain which makes its rare appearance in summer. Then the sudden realisation hit me like a thunderstorm striking in the backdrop of a beautiful sunny day.

How would he feel if he knew what had happened to me with "It"?

I was not pure and innocent like Humza thought I was. I suddenly felt sick in the stomach and wanted to just run away and be on my own. The euphoria had disintegrated to a deep mood of melancholy.

"Humza, I don't think you understand," I quickly said to cut the conversation short. I wanted to plan my escape back into my black hole, even though I knew it was filled with pain and sorrow.

What was I thinking? That someone as amazing as him would love me and for me to have that fairy tale life with him? Things like that just don't ever happen for me.

"What is there to understand? I love you and want to be with you! And from the vibe I was getting from you five minutes ago, you felt the same!" he said in a convincing tone.

"I don't know what you're on about. I must go," I quickly said as I stood up, getting ready to walk away.

"Zahra, no wait please we need to talk about this. Help me understand," he pleaded as I tried to go.

Humza grabbed my arm gently, captivating

my eyes intimately with his as I looked up at him slightly annoyed that he was trying to stop me.

Then he said, "Please hear me out. I have never felt like this about anyone. Ever. I am just as scared as you are, but we can't ignore this and we need to talk about it."

Humza guided me back towards the seats and we both sat down again.

"I would rather talk about this than just say no and ignore what we feel about each other. There is no going back from something like this. I don't want to risk losing you. One way or another I want you in my life because, I truly can't imagine my life without you. I realised this while you suddenly went missing without notice and you didn't come to uni," Humza said with concern in his voice.

I took a long deep breath as I prepared myself to speak. Heart still pounding again but this time not out of happiness as I said, "I, I don't know what to say."

As my eyes began to tear up, with a heavy heart I said, "I come from a family that will never accept this. You were born here, Humza—you have no idea what my parents are like. Particularly my mother. She is a traditional Afghan mother with very conservative and traditional ideas about marriage."

As I felt Humza's hand gently touching the side of my cheek, wiping away my tears, I abruptly drew back slightly. It was an unconscious action, a sudden reflex. No man had ever touched my face before, apart from Bahba.

Humza's reaction to this appeared in the form of an innocent smile and he said, "Sorry, I didn't mean to make you feel uncomfortable."

I managed to smile back but deep down knew this must be due to my childhood trauma with, you know, "It." I was uncomfortable with another's touch, especially from someone of the opposite gender. I was learning that this was a trauma response which manifested in my body twitching or falling into a sudden fight or flight mode, whereas other people probably wouldn't react in the same way.

"No, it's okay. You see Humza, there is no way my mother will accept this! Especially after what happened with Aunty Inji. My family have been through so much recently and I don't want to put them through any more pain." I managed to say this even though in my heart and mind I wanted to embrace Humza tightly and to tell him that I wanted this too, more than anything in the world!

I could read the hurt in Humza's eyes.

"I can imagine that this would be very hard for

your family to deal with right now with everything that happened with your Aunty, and I respect them for being so traditional. That is why I am more than happy to wait for the right moment to tell them about how we feel," he said persuasively.

"But Humza, I don't want you to place your life on hold for me when you have so many women keen on you. And bear in mind that they could still say no even if the time is right," I said as my thoughts went to Mother and how she would respond to this with the whole *faisha* dialogue—her go-to comeback when it comes to anything involving me. This would no doubt seal her argument.

Humza smiled back in response.

"I would happily wait for you for as long as you need. Yes, there are others very keen, and may I remind you also exceptionally beautiful women!" he said with a cheeky smile. "But my heart is set on my one and only—you. I will convince them that I am the right person for you. No matter how long it takes," he said as his face flushed pink.

Humza had no idea what he was getting himself into. Dealing with my family, particularly convincing my mother, would be like climbing Mount Everest and then, once you're up there, dealing with an oncoming tornado.

"I want this to remain a secret between us. Please don't tell anyone. Particularly anyone from our community. If this comes out before we discuss it with our parents, everything will go south quickly," I explained.

"Of course. My lips are permanently sealed until you say so," he said as he raised his hand and made a zipping motion across his mouth.

"However, there is one dilemma," he said.

"My brother already knows about you, and he knows exactly how I feel. I told him about you as soon as I developed these strong feelings towards you."

I must have looked crestfallen, so he went on quickly. "It's okay, as the good thing with Idris is that he hardly ever socialises in our community circles or functions like I do. He is what we would call an outcast. So, our secret will be safe," he said reassuringly.

Humza stood there for several seconds gazing at me as I did the same, feeling myself increasingly lost in his eyes. I wasn't sure what was happening just then, but I felt like I was floating on a light, fluffy cloud held delicately by his gaze.

Chapter 29

"*Salam*", I said as I kissed Grandmother's hand and sat next to her on the sofa.

"*Walekum asalam,* my beautiful girl," Grandmother said, ever so gently in reply.

"What has brought about this beautiful smile to my girl's face, I wonder?" Grandmother asked unexpectedly.

Nothing went unnoticed with Grandmother—she seemed to know everything without even a word being said.

I could feel my heart gaining speed, building up momentum. *Has Grandmother found out about Humza?* I wondered, feeling slightly panicked. *She can't have! No one knows about it. It has been several months now, but we have been incredibly careful not to show any signs of how we feel towards each other in public. And we haven't told anyone either. It has been so hard keeping this a secret from everyone, especially from Aunt Inji.*

I didn't like keeping secrets from my family. It

felt like I was doing something wrong by going behind their backs. I guess I was in a way. I was in love with Humza and wanted to marry him but hadn't told them. I felt conflicted. But why did I feel guilty about being in love? I was not doing anything *haram* or sacrilegious. Yes, I was talking to him, and we were spending time together, but we were still getting to know each other.

I am doing a little bit of flirting here and there, that's all. We are having lots of deep conversations about the future and our aspirations. We just want to discover whether we are compatible.

"Whatever it is, I love seeing you like this my girl, happy and glowing!" Grandmother said with a beautiful velvety smile.

Is it starting to show on my face? I thought for a moment. *I have been rather more upbeat and I have felt so much happier since Humza confessed his love for me, that is a fact.*

As Grandmother handed me her hairbrush to groom her long thinning mane, she curiously asked, "How are your studies going my girl?"

"They're going well Grandmother. I want to quickly finish my degree and start with the practical side of shadowing a doctor in the hospital to really get into it," I replied as I put the brush down next to me and started to plait her hair.

"Okay good. It's Allah's grace that you have such a blessed opportunity to study and fulfill your dreams. I am so glad that as an Afghan girl you can attain success. I am very much proud of you my girl," she said with praising words.

"Thank you Grandmother *jhan!* I would not be where I am if it wasn't for your prayers and Mother and Bahba's support and most of all, Aunt Inji's help," I said in reply, because it was true, I was incredibly grateful for their support and encouragement.

"Ah yes, your Aunt Inji is a wonderful inspiration. But remember—in life we live, and we learn. Not only from our own mistakes and experiences but also from mistakes of those around us," Grandmother said.

I wasn't sure what Grandmother was referring to, but I loved listening to her wise words, full of inspiration and experience.

"You see your Aunt Inji is a unique and wise woman. She is intelligent, beautiful, and successful! But her greatest weakness is her inability to sometimes push past the barriers that society erects, particularly more so for us women," Grandmother said as she turned around and held my hand, gesturing me to pause for a moment, ensuring she had my full attention.

"That marriage to Omar was her greatest downfall and mistake. And all in the name of culture. She didn't know the man well enough to make such a big decision to marry him," she said.

"I mean what is the rush? But at the same time, I don't agree with making love with every man that says they like you," Grandmother said.

Grandmother's quaint use of the term, "making love" is how we'd say "making out" these days, I thought with amusement and affection.

"A woman's affection is her gold, and she needs to make sure she spends it sparingly and wisely on a man who is truly deserving," she continued with a gentle smile and a wink to seal it off.

I could not help but giggle at her and said, "What has got into you, I am now worried about you!"

Grandmother laughed as she let go of my hand and turned her head around allowing me to continue with the braid.

"All I am saying, my girl, is that yes, it is wonderful that you are studying to become a doctor and securing your future, but this alone is not the definition of success! True success is when you also have someone nice to share your life with and someone to grow old with—tackling this adventure called life together!" Grandmother said wisely.

"Oh Grandmother, I don't have time for all that," I quickly replied.

"Come on my girl. You are young and beautiful, make sure you keep your eyes peeled and if anyone handsome fancies those beautiful eyes of yours, then don't be afraid to let your heart flutter towards them and explore the possibilities. Of course, within the limits of your religion and family values!" Grandmother said as she led out a long loud laugh.

I was shocked by Grandmother's statement. It was almost as if she knew about Humza already and was giving me the green light to go ahead and marry him!

"Seriously, what has got into you, Grandmother!" I managed to say as I secured the end of Grandmother's braid with a hair tie.

This was exactly what I needed to hear! Grandmother's approval meant the world to me. Also, knowing that someone else was on my side who would back me up when I did speak with Mother and Bahba, was great!

"What is all this laughter? You, Grandmother and granddaughter, what are you up to now?" Mother said as she entered the room with a tray of food for Grandmother.

I got up and was now standing directly in front of Grandmother and next to Mother as she held the tray of food in her hand staring at us both.

“Nothing just Grandmother and granddaughter chatter!” Grandmother said with a secretive veil over her eyes as she smiled, nodding her head and winking at me as she reassured me that she meant every word she had just uttered.

“I’d better get back to my studies,” I said nervously.

* * *

My bedroom was my safe space. My room and my studies! I tried not to get in the way of Mother, as I could sense she was still very unhappy with the suitor situation and the fact that Aunt Inji was able to convince Mother to let me return to uni. As much as I was grateful for this, I was walking on eggshells with Mother and didn’t want to ruffle any feathers or cause an upset. But the guilt I carried was heavy! I had been trusted to return to uni and focus on my studies but the situation with Humza was brewing in the back of my mind like a gathering storm.

I knew that I needed to let them know about Humza at some point. It would be a great weight off my shoulders for sure. However, I was aware that it would be seen as such a grave breach of trust for going behind their backs. Deep down, I knew that if they just gave Humza a chance, they would no doubt love him just as I did.

Look at me, I thought, *fantasising about me and Humza like it is a sealed deal! First of all, if Mother has anything to do with it, it will remain just that—a fantasy. Secondly, I have this big dirty secret, the abuse from "It" that is always weighing on my mind. It's something I can't out-think or forget about, and I must, at all costs, keep it to myself.*

Maybe Humza will see it for what it is, child abuse, with him being more open minded and so understanding. But it could also go the other way, I could lose him forever and the community could find out. Then not only will I risk losing Humza, but also my family and respect in the community. What a heavy burden, like a life sentence for a crime in which I am the victim. Now I know how those people feel when they have been wrongly accused or convicted of a crime, I thought.

Chapter 30

I was appreciating the lovely weather and taking in the fresh scent of the eucalyptus leaves in the breeze. The sky above me was a beautiful light blue, with white fluffy clouds that seemed to take shapes of their own—morphing into different silhouettes. At one point I thought I saw a lion with a large white mane. Such tranquillity.

I couldn't believe another year was coming to an end. The second year of Med school had been extremely stressful, particularly with the Physics unit, which by God's grace and Humza's support, I had managed to pass.

It had been eight months now since Humza had told me how he felt about me. We tried to spend as much time together as possible. I needed to be sure about him and find out for certain whether he was someone I could truly spend the rest of my life with. This was the first big decision I had made in my life of my own accord, so I needed to be sure that he was the one.

"What are you daydreaming about, Pretty Eyes?" Humza asked as we sat down with our backs leaning against the large eucalyptus tree, near the university library.

"Nothing, just appreciating the beautiful sky putting on such a beautiful show on this fine day," I said as I looked across at him sitting next to me.

How did I get so lucky? To have someone as amazing as him wanting to be with me!

I loved it when he referred to me as "Pretty Eyes," which is something he did often. I did sometimes wonder, though, if he would feel the same if he knew about, you know, "It" and what he did to me. Would he be dismayed to know about the abuse, and think that I was damaged goods, who no one wants?

My mind returned to the question Humza had addressed to "Pretty Eyes," He was gazing at me, waiting for my answer.

"Oh nothing, you calling me 'Pretty Eyes' just reminded me of something," I said as I quickly changed my train of thought, ensuring that what I was truly thinking about was not at all evident in my facial expression.

"Please do share. I'd love to know what you are reminded of when I call you 'Pretty Eyes', he said.

"Well, I have always had a nickname for you since our first days of uni. Which I've never told you about," I said in a lightly shy tone. *That was a good save*, I thought. *I'm not usually good like that, quick on my toes with my responses.*

"Oh really! This is the first time I'm hearing about this. I'm dying to know!" Humza said with lots of wonder and excitement.

"I don't know, it's embarrassing,"I said sheepishly as I giggled like a school child.

"Come on! I'll try and not laugh, I promise," Humza said in a rather desperate tone.

"Okay, hummm my nickname for you is … is

… Mister Fluffy," I said and quickly raised my hands and covered my eyes out of sheer shyness.

All I could hear was Humza's loud laugh as I slowly pulled my hands away from my eyes. There I saw him giggling uncontrollably.

"Okay do explain the theory behind this nickname!" he managed to say in between the bursts of laughter. "Are you suggesting that I'm fat and fluffy!" he asked, continuing to laugh hysterically.

I couldn't help but to laugh too now as I managed to say, "No of course not! It's because…" then paused. I was feeling very nervous revealing my inner thoughts about him.

As I looked up at Humza, he was now looking deeply into my eyes, captivating all my emotions, encouragingly allowing me the space to reveal my true feelings.

"Because to me, you are dreamy like a fluffy cloud I guess," I managed to say softly.

Humza leaned over, touched my hand and held it in his. Instantly, shivers ran down my spine. Then touched the side of my cheek as he softly said, "I wonder how incredible it would be to kiss you on the hand and then your face."

I quickly snatched my hand out of his. I felt the temptation of wanting the same but I was so conflicted. Part of me felt like I was being dirty to want to be kissed by Humza, but the other part of me was taken back to when, you know, "It" abused me as a child. Deep down I knew that they were two different scenarios but in that intimate moment when Humza tried to hold my hand or touch my face, the fear rushes through my body and the guilt is overwhelming.

"I am sorry Zahra; I can't help how I feel. I know we have spoken about this at length, and I respect your decision but this crazy heart of mine can't control itself!" he said as he looked down, with a melancholy expression on his face.

I knew that I was not doing anything wrong—Humza was just expressing how he felt about me and innocently holding my hand—but the fact that we were not engaged, and my family didn't know about him also really bothered me. We had spoken about this, and he knew how I felt and respected my boundaries and family values. I knew that at times like this he struggled with abiding by these limitations.

The heart wants what the heart wants! I thought.

"No don't apologise." I smiled at Humza in sympathy. "I did warn you from day one that my life was complicated and dealing with my family would not be easy. They are very traditional," I added.

"Maybe it's time I spoke with Aunt Inji about us. She is the most reasonable person in my entire family! And my brother Imran, he's also very understanding and open minded," I said as I fidgeted with my bracelet, moving it from side to side in a rhythmic motion.

"I think Grandmother secretly knows about us somehow! I hope at least she will give us her blessing and support," I said excitedly as I turned to face Humza.

"What do you mean, did you tell your grandmother?" Humza asked with a confused expression on his face.

"Recently she pulled me aside and was telling me about keeping my eyes peeled for a handsome man to marry and grow old with. And not in terms of arranged marriage but actual love marriage! I'm still in shock," I said, still with a tone of disbelief in my voice.

"Well, your grandmother rocks! She is definitely talking about me!" Humza said as he chuckled. His laugh was so contagious, I couldn't help but join in with him.

"You're too much!" I said as I playfully pushed his arm.

"Okay jokes aside, I like the idea of speaking with Aunt Inji and getting her approval first and then we can maybe talk to Grandmother and then work towards convincing your mother and Bahba. Because my love, there is only so much self-control a man can have when he has such beauty sitting right next to him!" Humza said as he knelt, his face close to mine.

"Yes, Mister Romantic! We know, we know," I said as I gently pushed him back and stood up.

"I know we need to do something. We can't sit on it forever but I want to make sure I have enough fight in me to be able to weather the storm with Mother," I said with concern about what was yet to come.

"Come on, I am sure everything will be fine! Once your mother sees this face, she won't have a choice but to adore me!" Humza said with a wild grin on his face.

Humza is so innocent and naive, I thought. *He has no understanding of Mother and her wrath. Maybe I should prepare him for the struggles that lie ahead with my family, in particular Mother. I wonder, does he have it in him to make it through this? What if he gives up on us and runs the other direction after meeting Mother!*

"Humza, I know I have said this before, but my family is very traditional, and Mother is a hard one to get through to. I want you to know that any point you feel like it is not worth the fight then it is okay to back down. We can remain friends," I said.

My thoughts were slipping into a fog of hopelessness. *Mother already thinks the worst of me, so can't even imagine what this will do. In her eyes I am an utter disappointment.*

"Hey, hey. I am not having any of that. I love you Zahra and nothing can change that. No amount of turmoil that you, your mother or your entire family can put me through will change that. So please stop with that line of thought immediately," Humza said as he stood up and gently reached for my hands and held them in his.

"So long as you still want me in your life, I am willing to go through anything. But we need to stay united—no matter how bad it gets and never turn against each other. Because if we do, that will be the end of us!" he said as he passionately held my eyes in his.

How is it possible that someone cares about me so much? I don't know how all this happened, but I am so grateful that I have Humza's love. It gives me hope and strength for the future.

"I hope so Humza. I am so scared that things will get so messed up, that I will never see you again," I said in an overly concerned tone.

"Can I give you a quick hug? The moment is so perfect for me to hold you in my arms," Humza said passionately.

"No Romeo! I am here worrying my heart out and all you can think of is hugging," I said as I pulled my hands out of his.

"What about your family? How do you think your mother and Bahba feel about all this?" I asked in a concerned yet curious tone.

"Well, I have told my brother and he is supportive as always. As with mum and dad I think they will be happy and feel relieved that I have brought home an Afghan girl for marriage!" Humza said as he burst into laughter.

I couldn't help but laugh along with him. How easy he had it in life! It was all so simple with very few restraints or conditions. That was exactly how I wanted to live.

"No Humza, I'm being serious!" I said in a frustrated tone.

"My parents are very easy-going, Zahra. They have been living in this country for an exceptionally long time now. All they want from me is to be a good person, stay close to my religion and to marry an Afghan!" he said.

"So, I am really sure that my parents, particularly my mother, will adore you. She always wanted to have a daughter and now she will," he said with lots of confidence and a smile to accompany it.

Chapter 31

It feels so good—telling someone who is especially important person in my life about Humza, it is like having a huge weight lifted off my chest. At least for now!

"I am so happy for you princess! When can I meet him?" Aunt Inji asked, laughing with excitement as she stood jumping on the spot holding my hands in hers.

"Whenever you want. I am just really worried about Mother and Bahba. Especially Mother, you know what she's like," I said in a concerned tone as she stopped jumping and stood still with my hand still in hers.

"It's okay princess, we will figure it out together. One thing I want to know. Are you sure he is a good and decent person who deserves you?" she asked as her eyes teared up like two lakes, preparing to overflow.

I forget how difficult this must be for Aunty Inji. It must bring back traumatic memories about Uncle Omar.

"I think so. He is very down to earth, kind, and easy going. I mean, he seems to think the world of me and really respects me," I said in his support.

"Why wouldn't he, princess! You truly are a package with beauty and brains!" she said excitedly.

"I don't know about that. But I am worried about Mother and how she will react to this. One thing I am sure of is that it won't be pleasant," I said with tone of disappointment.

"Zahra, take a deep breath, we will work this out. First things first, who else from the family knows about this?" Aunt Inji asked inquisitively.

"No one knows. The only person that knows is Humza's brother," I quickly replied.

"Why do you ask, Aunt Inji?" I queried.

"Humza, I like that name!" she digressed. "The reason is simple. Your parents are old fashioned, so we need to bear that in mind and approach the matter accordingly," Aunt Inji said as she stood up and paced back and forth with her hand on her chin in deep concentration.

"What are you thinking Aunt Inji? You are now totally freaking me out," I said, my levels of anxiety starting to build.

"I am thinking, don't tell Mother or Bahba about Humza or how you feel about him for now," she said calculatingly.

"Let his parents come for *khasgaree* and pretend that it is the first time you two have met! They get what they want—an arranged marriage—and you get what you want, to marry the love of your life! Problem solved!" Aunt Inji said as she clapped her hands in excitement.

On the surface the idea sounds brilliant but I really don't want to lie to Mother.

"I don't know Aunt Inji, I don't like the idea of lying to Mother. It always has a way of coming out and blowing up in my face and making the situation worst," I said pessimistically.

"Okay so will you walk up and say to her, 'Mother I am in love and want to marry this boy Humza'? What do you think will happen? That she will give you her blessing? You are dreaming my girl!" Aunt Inji said sarcastically.

"Once things progress, you might be engaged or even married by the time the truth comes out, and when it does, we can deal with it accordingly," Aunt Inji said convincingly.

Mother already thinks I am a faisha and this will make her believe that even more! I will never outlive this label if I marry Humza. This is all so overwhelming!

My head was spinning just thinking about it.

"Aunt Inji, I have never made any big decisions on my own in my life! I have so much self-doubt and I keep second guessing myself," I said in a worried tone.

"Look princess, don't overthink it. I'm sure we will figure it out. Trust your heart and your judgment. I promise I have your back, always! But let's get back to the exciting part, I want to meet him—like right now!" she said with the wave of excitement returning.

"Of course! Whenever you like," I said, trying to reciprocate Aunt Inji's excitement. "But please keep it strictly between us! Not a word to anyone, especially Mother."

"Princess, you know you can trust me. I won't say a word until and unless you want me to," Aunt Inji said convincingly as she came close and held my face in her hands, aligning our eyes to reassure me.

"I know Aunt Inji, it's just that I am worried about Mother and don't want to disappoint her anymore," I said as I gazed straight into her eyes.

"But I can take you now to meet him if you like. He works part-time at a local men's clothing shop," I said.

"Oh goodness! Yes, let's go now," Aunt Inji said,

looking thrilled.

Before I knew it, Aunt Inji had grabbed my wrist and was tugging me out the door.

* * *

Humza nervously greeted Aunt Inji. "*Salaams,* nice to finally meet you. I've heard so many amazing things about you," he said as he gently shook her hand.

"Well *Salaams*, to you too! I hope you've heard only the good things about me," Aunt Inji said as Humza laughed nervously.

"I tell you what, I see exactly why my beautiful niece is crazy about you!" Aunt Inji said staring at Humza with a sheepish smile.

I nudged her on the arm gently signalling her to stop embarrassing me as she turned her head slightly towards me and made an expression with her mouth saying something like "so fine" accompanied by a wink.

I was so nervous and could feel my face flushing red. Ambushing Humza without warning wasn't the ideal way of making introductions. We had spoken about letting Aunt Inji know about us but not exactly like this. He was surprised but appeared to be handling the situation rather well.

"So young man, what are your intentions with

my niece?" she asked him like he was in a police interrogation.

I was feeling slightly on edge while this was unfolding in front of me, even though it was going well so far. I couldn't even imagine how I would be if this was Mother or Bahba, and I was in Humza's place right now!

"I love Zahra and want to marry her and spend the rest of our lives together. I have never met anyone like her," he said as he looked over his shoulder to catch a glimpse of my face and reaction.

As I caught his eyes I smiled and shyly lowered my gaze.

"Humza, our Zahra is one of a kind! She has a line of suitors, but what makes you different to all those other eligible bachelors?" Aunt Inji asked as she smirked some more. I felt like she was taking this lightly and not being as serious as I thought she would be. Which was working in Humza's favour I guess—less pressure on him.

But as I looked up at Humza, I could see the colour rising in his cheeks as he responded, "Yes, Zahra is truly one of a kind. What sets me apart from all the other suitors is that Zahra over time has really got to know me as a person, so I am not some stranger."

He continued, "She knows that I love her and would do anything to keep her happy and support her to make her dreams come true. I honestly don't think I am good enough for her and think she deserves better than me but what can I do? My heart is locked in her hands," Humza said genuinely.

"I like your response! Okay you passed that test with excellence!" Aunt Inji said as she turned to look at me with approval. I don't know what has got into her today. But I like seeing her so happy and excited after so long.

I am on cloud nine after hearing Humza speak so beautifully about me! I never thought I would experience this. To feel loved and wanted and for someone to see so much good in me—it is like being in a dream.

Chapter 32

The heat of the sand gently touched the skin on my feet. It felt warm and soothing as I walked towards the oncoming waves. As the water touched my feet, it washed away the heat from the sun and left my feet feeling refreshed.

The serenity of Bondi Beach was unmatched—the crisp fresh air, the invigorating water coloured in beautiful shades of blue and turquoise with silver lining of white along the way.

Such untouched beauty is food for the soul, I thought.

Bondi beach was Humza's and my go-to meeting place outside uni. With so many tourists around, it allowed us to blend in effortlessly, giving us the veil of privacy to get to know each other better.

"When will you stop laughing so much about Aunt Inji's interrogation! I get it, I was mumbling and nervous but what do you expect after being put on the spot like that?" he was still slightly recovering from the trauma of the other day when Aunty Inji had paid him a surprise visit.

"Okay sorry, no more teasing Mister Nice guy! Are you ready for tonight? Is everything in order at your end?" I asked as my tone changed from teasing to slightly more composed.

"Yes, I have my suit. My parents are ready and dad will leave work early to make sure we get to your house on time. But I am so nervous Zahra," Humza said as he bent down and picked up a pearly white shell, rubbing the sand off it. This is unlike him, he is usually the carefree, positive one.

"What if your parents don't like me or approve? I am going in with the idea that we will be engaged and married soon after tonight. There is no space in my mind or heart about any other alternatives. What happens if they say 'no'. Will I ever see you again?" he asked in a concerned tone.

Humza had just pointed out the thing that has been burdening me the most the past couple of days. There is some comfort knowing that I am not the only one.

"I know what you mean Humza, the same worry has haunted me for days," I said.

"For me, I am in this 1000%! No matter what. We will convince your parents—no matter how long it takes," he said determinedly.

"So am I Humza, if my parents reject the

relationship there is not much I can do. There is expectation on me as a female to make sacrifices, something I have learnt and adapted to from a young age," I said as I looked down at the sand as it dispersed itself in between my toes.

"What does that mean Zahra? That you will sacrifice our love and your own happiness just to keep everyone else happy? Where is the logic in that," Humza said in a frustrated tone as he came to a halt.

"Humza, where I come from logic is not the basis of decision making. I want you to know that I am not the type of person who can live happily ever after, while my family is upset and in turmoil because of my actions," I quickly replied.

"What about us and what we feel for each other? You won't fight for us, for our love or our future?" he asked desperately.

"Of course I will! That is not what I am saying. I am just being a realist and considering the possibility that things may not turn out the way we have pictured it in our minds," I said in a melancholy tone.

"I am just worried that you may underestimate how difficult things may get and I would understand if at any point this became all too much and you wanted to walk away," I said.

"Hey, we are in this together, no matter how long it takes! I only see myself with you and no other person. From my end you need not worry at all. I will wait for you forever if that is what it takes to make sure you become my wife! My only concern is that you will buckle under pressure and will give up on us," Humza said, looking downcast.

"I wish I could give you that kind of solid commitment. I want to be with you more than anything. But you don't know my family and how complicated they can be. Especially when they are angry and feel their cultural beliefs and ideas are being undermined," I said as I bent down to touch the warm sand with my fingers.

"To them, arranged marriages are all they know. So, I understand where they are coming from, even though I don't agree with the logic as it is outdated and clearly doesn't work," I said as I released the sand gradually through my fingers.

"See this response of yours freaks me out! Makes me feel hopeless," Humza said disheartedly.

"Humza, I am sorry, I don't want to sugar coat the situation. I am being honest with you. I will put up a fight for us, but I won't walk over my parents or break their hearts just for my own happiness," I said with a sad tone. "To me that would be being selfish, but you may think I am weak," I managed to say as I felt a wave of emotion take over me.

"Zahra, this is exactly why I love you so much! There is this veil of innocence, an abundance of kindness in you and selflessness that I have never witnessed in anyone else," Humza said as he stepped closer towards me and took my hand in his hand. He gently touched the side of my cheek with his other hand.

I did not flinch.

"As you know I am not one who is overtly religious but at this very moment in time I surrender myself and our relationship to God and pray that he helps us fight this battle and that we come out victorious," he said sincerely.

It was nice to hear that Humza could finally understand a little of what it was like for me. But I wondered if he was really prepared for the storm that was ahead. But hearing him talk so passionately really made me fall more in love with him than ever!

If I could find any fault at all in Humza, it would be that he was not as close to Islam as I would want him to be. But I knew that religion was a subjective journey for each person, no matter what their background or life experience.

I pray to God that this test brings him even closer to God and that he can excel in this journey, strengthening his faith.

Chapter 33

I opened my bedroom door slightly so that I could see into the living room. I saw Humza sitting nervously, and next to him a middle-aged woman in elegant attire and make up—I assumed this was his mother. My heart was pounding with anticipation. I couldn't see further into the living room beyond that angle but, luckily, I was able to hear nearly everything. Things were moving beyond the greeting stage, and they were now getting into the serious conversation about the *khasgaree*.

"We apologise for inconveniencing you today with our presence, but we wanted to discuss our humble proposal for your lovely daughter Zahra's hand in marriage with our son Humza," I heard the male voice say and guessed it to be that of Humza's Bahba.

"I have heard lovely things about your family and your daughter from our small community here in Western Sydney and it would be an honour for me and my family to have your daughter join our family as my daughter-in-law. And I know as a parent you must have a thousand questions and concerns, which is understandable," the deep male voice continued.

"Thank you for your kind words," I heard Mother respond.

The questions continued, noticeably with more questions from Mother and Bahba than from Humza's parents. Mother didn't leave any stone unturned when it came to Humza. She asked him what his goal for the next five years was and he responded well, in my opinion. After all, this was something he and I had discussed numerous times. To finish Med school and get hands-on experience at a local hospital and start working on building our medical careers with the hope of one day opening our own medical practice. Mother and Bahba sounded incredibly positive about knowing that Humza was also in medical school studying to become a doctor.

I felt a slight ease in tension come over me as I eavesdropped on those snippets of their conversation. It was all heading in a positive direction. I gently closed my bedroom door and did a quick victory dance around my room. *Yay, yay!*

Soon afterwards, I heard them leave. They had

only stayed for a noticeably fleeting period, but Mother said that with *khasgaree*, it can take a guy's family several visits before the girl's family says either "yes" or rejects the proposal. Then if the girl's family are leaning towards saying "yes," they will allow the girl to come into the room and serve everyone tea. Then she would be able to get a glimpse of the guy in the process. Then in the proceeding visits there might be an opportunity for the young people to speak with each other.

As I heard footsteps coming towards my bedroom door, I quickly ran back to my desk and pretended to be deep in study mode with exams just around the corner.

"That's my good girl," Bahba said as he partially opened my bedroom door seeing me draped over my books.

"My dear Zahra, I want to talk to you about something very important," Bahba said in a calm voice.

"Yes, sure Bahba come in," I said as I closed my Physics textbook.

Bahba sat down at the edge of my bed facing me with his hands cuffed together on his lap. He looked up at me and said, "Zahra you are the apple of my eye. I am so proud that I have such an amazing daughter like you."

He looked down while fidgeting with his fingers, like he was gathering the strength to say something important. Of course, I knew what it was about but did my best not to give it away.

"I know you made it clear that you didn't want to get married and that you want to focus on your studies, and I respect that and love you for prioritising your studies above all. But my child, opportunity doesn't always come knocking," Bahba said as he looked up at me with a warm smile.

"As Mother has mentioned to you, we had a potential suitor, and his family came over earlier. Before you jump up and down in protest, hear me out," Bahba said as he noticed my facial expression change.

To my surprise, this time Mother had mentioned to me, ahead of time, that a suitor was coming.

"There was something about this man and his family that really sat well with me in my heart. It didn't make me feel like I was giving you away but rather gaining another family member to love and take care of you, when we are no longer around," Bahba said humbly.

My eyes welled up with love. I had rehearsed this but not this part where I would get so emotional.

Bahba's raw emotions and the reality of getting married was sinking in. This was something that I had not factored in. Hearing such kind words felt foreign, but it was so nice that my feelings could not be held back.

As the tears trundled down the side of my face, Bahba lovingly wiped them away with the back of his hands, as his eyes began to moisten too.

"What are you doing Zahra! You are going to make me end up in tears too," Bahba said as he reached out and held me in his arms.

I was a complete mess! I couldn't control myself. The validation that, for once in my life, I had made the right decision by picking Humza was overwhelming. It seemed that Mother and Bahba were good judges of character, and they too saw in him what I saw the first time I met him.

I wished I could just come out and tell Bahba that I knew Humza, that I thought he was amazing and that I couldn't wait till they got to know him like I did! I was sure they would love him just as much as I did.

"This suitor's name is Humza. He too is in medical school like you. In fact, he is in the same uni as you! What are the chances of this happening, right?" Bahba said excitedly as he continued to embrace me tightly.

I nodded my head in agreement. It felt so wrong lying to Bahba. It went against every ounce of my being!

"Mother, Grandmother, and I truly feel he is the right one to keep you happy and safe. Even though this is the first time they have come for *khasgaree*, my heart is already leaning towards a 'yes'!" Bahba said.

"I can see that they seem more conformed to the social norms of this country, but they have somehow managed to still keep our traditions and culture alive," he continued.

"Grandmother has suggested that at the next visit you should come and meet him, talk to him and see how you feel about him," Bahba said.

"We are not saying you have to say 'yes' but to give it thoughtful consideration. My dear, chances like this are rare. Like a sunrise, if you wait too long, you might miss it," he said as he gently moved me away from his chest to get a glimpse of my face.

"Now what do you say?" he asked as he was looking at me, teary eyed with a soft smile.

"Okay Bahba," is all I managed to say.

What should been a joyous moment had been overshadowed by the lie that I was now harbouring.

Like when there is a beautiful rainbow draping across the sky, only to be overshadowed by rain sprinkling overhead in the skies above.

I can't wait to speak with Humza on Monday to find out exactly what was discussed and how things unfolded. Even though Bahba seemed positive, we needed to make sure that it stayed that way.

As Bahba left the room, Aunt Inji made her way into the room with a poker face on. She closed the door and her face changed to a contented smile. She hugged me as we both remained embraced, giggling slightly, but conscious of not making too much noise.

Chapter 34

"Bye Mother, I'm going to uni. Imran is dropping me off. See you later tonight," I shouted out as I left the house.

Everyone in the house seemed to be in such good spirits since the *khasgaree*, even Mother! I couldn't believe this was happening. So much happiness in my life, and all at once, was unheard of. I even overheard Bahba last night saying he has heard of Humza's family in the community and has only heard positive things about them.

This made me even more paranoid that something bad would happen to destroy everything! As the feeling of anxiety about the truth coming out haunted me, seeing Humza near the uni entry gave me a sense of hope. He ran towards me and without any thought just grabbed me around the waist, lifting me off the ground before spinning me around like a mannequin.

"It went well! Zahra we will be together forever, just like we dreamed!" Humza said as he continued spinning me around.

“Yeah, okay. Put me down please, we’re not engaged yet!” I managed to say as he slowly lowered me back down.

“I can’t believe it worked!” Humza said excitedly. Noticing that I was not sharing the same enthusiasm, he asked, “You are not having second thoughts about me, are you, ‘Pretty eyes’?”

“Of course not, silly! I am just anxious about the lie. I keep thinking Mother will find out and everything will backfire,” I promptly replied anxiously.

“Zahra, you are such a pessimist! We had no other choice. It was either this or die pining for one another,” he said as he smiled and gently nudged me in the shoulder. I returned a small smile while shaking my head in disapproval.

I loved this about him. He could cheer me up no matter what was bringing me down.

“Let’s go to the cafeteria. We can get some energy drinks and something to eat and talk about the *kasgree*,” he said excitedly.

I couldn’t help but laugh out loud hysterically as he butchered the word *‘khasgaree’!* His pronunciation of the Dari language was terrible. This was something I hoped to be able to help him with.

"What did I say? Okay yeah, you do that laugh at the Oz boy's atrocious pronunciation!" he said as he followed me into the cafeteria.

"Einstein, it is pronounced *khasgaree!* What is it with you Australians—always wanting to abbreviate everything?" I said teasingly as I continued to giggle.

"Okay enough of this! Tell me everything. What did they ask and what was the vibe?" I asked, desperate to know what went down during the *khasgaree* (even though I had eavesdropped most of it and knew it went well!).

"Look, your parents asked questions that I would have asked as well if someone came asking for my daughter's hand. You have a lovely family who genuinely care about you and want the best for you," Humza said.

I do have a lovely family, but I don't agree that they want what is best for me. Rather, they want what works for them within the boundaries of my culture and community. It is funny how two people looking at the same situation can interpret it completely differently.

"I feel like my parents did well too and were open and honest. I was confident with my responses and respectful without stepping on any toes," he continued boastingly.

"Well, you must have done something right

because Bahba came and asked me to consider a 'yes' reply to the proposal as his heart is in it—or something to that affect," I eagerly replied.

"Really! No way!" Humza said as he jumped out of his seat in excitement.

"Oh my god! Calm down. Sit down, sit," I said as I noticed all eyes from the café were on us now.

"I love you Zahra! I knew we would end up together," he said as he sat down, reaching out and placing his hands on the back of my hand and squeezing it gently.

"I can't wait till I can hold you in my arms and kiss your face. To plan the rest of our lives together! Mrs Dr and Mr Dr coming right at you! You'd better prepare for our amazing love and life story!" Humza said in a heightened emotional tone.

I began to blush and could feel hint of pink taking over my cheeks. Usually, when someone touched me on the shoulder or anywhere, I was jumpy and anxious. But I have recently noticed a change, in that I feel shy but not jumpy like I used to.

I remembered reading an article about childhood sexual assault victims. It was about distrust of men and what the article referred to as PTSD, post-traumatic stress disorder. It actually helped me make sense of all the symptoms that I had been experiencing. But I felt like I was doing much better now with all the self-help reading I'd done and that it had got me to where I was now in this journey towards healing. The frequency of flashbacks, the horrible nightmares and the hypervigilance, to name a just a few symptoms that I have suffered throughout the years, have begun to reduce and actually feel like they have started to come under control.

Maybe it is finally my time to shine, have peace and maybe even be happy.

Chapter 35

Grandmother sat on my study chair as I gently untied her hair to prepare it for brushing. I carefully brushed her hair from top to bottom, using several strokes in a downward motion.

Grandmother's hair was white like the clouds above and it felt soft like silk in my hands as I plaited it. This was one of my favourite things to do for Grandmother, to plait her hair. I also liked preparing her favourite Afghan green tea with sugar cubes that she loved so much.

"You know my Zahra, I have seen it all in my lifetime. The good, the bad and the difficult. Listen well," Grandmother said as she turned her head slightly to face me. "Don't live life like you're holding on to it, but rather live it like you're passing it by," she said.

I didn't really know what she meant by this. It was yet another wise statement from Grandmother that I needed months to ponder over to really understand. She truly was a fountain of knowledge and wisdom.

"I wish someone had said this to me when I was your age. Hindsight is a superpower that I would pick if I had the choice," she continued.

I returned Grandmother a thoughtful smile.

Before I could say anything I heard the entry door slam. Then I heard Mother, yelling and screaming. I quickly tied Grandmother's hair and made my way to the living room to see what all the commotion was about.

"Get out of my sight you *faisha!* Get out before I lose it and break your head open!" Mother screamed in rage.

Suddenly my heart started beating like a drum without control. "What is it Mother? What's upset you so much?" I managed to ask.

"Cut out the innocent act. You may have fooled everyone else, but you will never fool me!" she said with pure fury.

Bahba ran into the room and wedged himself in between Mother and me as she pushed her way towards me in a fit of rage. I began to cry and scream.

The peace that had existed a few minutes ago seem like a distant mirage.

Grandmother came into the living room too. "What is it child? Sit down and for the sake of

God calm down and speak! You are not making any sense," she said with a tone of authority.

Mother, now crying finally sat down. Bahba handed her some tissues which she pressed in her hand like she was taking her rage out on the tissue before lifting it to wipe her nose.

"I have never been so embarrassed in my whole life! I wish you had died when I gave birth to you so I would not have to live to see this day Zahra," Mother said with so much hurt in her tone.

My heart was now beating so hard it was ready to leap out through my chest and my hands started to shake. I could feel my legs giving way.

Surely Mother could not have found out the truth about Humza and me? How did she know? My mind was in a turmoil.

"I was at the butchers just now and bumped into Soria's mother," Mother said as she continued to sniffle and cry.

"I mentioned the *khasgaree* to her and that is when she said, 'Good that the new generation are smart—they try before they buy,' saying that Zahra and Humza know each other from uni and are in love," she said, weeping inconsolably.

My heart sank deeper into the pit of my stomach. *Soria, that bitch!* I thought we were careful. We were so sure that no one would suspect us being together.

Bahba turned around to face me with accusing eyes while I could hear Mother wailing in the background. The disappointment in Bahba's eyes was breaking my heart. He was the one person I never ever wanted to disappoint.

"I promise Bahba, I haven't done anything to bring shame to you or my family," I pleaded desperately.

"So, this is true, you know Humza from university?" Bahba asked curiously.

As fear crept into me, I slowly stepped backwards landing on the couch.

"Yes Bahba, Humza goes to the same uni as me and is in most of my classes," I said as I lowered my head.

Bahba lowered his head as he sat on the couch opposite me. Mother, still crying, sat next to me.

I somehow gathered the strength to get up and sat on the floor in front of Bahba, my arms on his knee as I held his hand in mine. All the while the tears were rolling down my face like the Indian monsoon.

"I met him at Aunt Inji's wedding first and then at uni as he too is also studying medicine and that's where I got to know him better. But I promise you

I have not done anything to dishonour you, my religion or my culture," I pleaded in my defence.

"Do you love him Zahra?" Bahba asked as he gently raised my soaking chin with his hand to align my lowered gaze with his.

The stream of tears continued to flow down the sides of my face. My heart was heavy with pain and sadness as I held his disappointed gaze in mine.

"Bahba, I don't know what love is. But he respects me, cares about me, and understands that my goal in life is to become a doctor and to save lives," I managed to say.

"He knows that my family comes first, always more than anything else. If this is 'love' Bahba then yes, I am in love with him," I said as I lowered my head in shame.

Suddenly my whole body was in shock with pain radiating from my throat down to the tip of my toes. I quickly realised that Mother had grabbed me by the neck, pulling me backwards away from Bahba as she squeezed tightly, while continuing to scream profanities.

I couldn't breathe! I was struggling to take in any air.

"You *faisha!* I will not let you soil this family's name in shit along with you!" she screamed as she continued her grip on my neck squeezing and pulling me back with what seemed like both her hands. Mother was extraordinarily strong in her fury.

"Let her go! Stop it now!" Bahba yelled as he tried his hardest to release Mother's grip while I struggled to breathe.

Finally, Mother let go of my throat as she and Bahba collapsed on the couch exhausted from the ordeal, while I dropped in a heap on the floor gasping for air.

Imran had also come running into the room, a horrified expression on his face. Grandmother was still looking distressed too, with bloodshot red eyes.

I was still recovering from Mother's attack, gasping and coughing.

What am I doing to my family? I thought, *All for a man who may turn out to be a monster like most men I know.* As this thought demonised me from the inside I managed to get up and ran into my bedroom slamming the door shut behind me.

Chapter 36

Last night's events left me feeling totally incapacitated, both physically and mentally. My throat felt sore and my voice was raspy. I had some pain when swallowing. I was emotionally drained and I didn't have the courage to return to the living room or see any of them ever again! The level of shame I had yet again brought over this family was incomprehensible. I wished I was dead instead.

"I knew there was something different about my Zahra, lately. She seemed more vibrant," I could hear Grandmother say as I sat leaning on the back of my locked bedroom door.

Was Grandmother defending me? I was confused. I held my ear closer to the door to hear more clearly. My heart started to pound again within my chest like a bomb ticking away minutes before an explosion.

I had spent most of last night in tears. I didn't think I had any more tears left in me. *What a mess my life is!* I thought.

But this was a small glimpse of daylight for me. For Grandmother to still love me after learning the truth about me and Humza, when my own Mother despised me, was a testimony to how much Grandmother understood and loved me.

"What are you on about Mother?" I heard Mother say in reply, sounding slightly irritated.

"You know, not everything has to be said out loud. Some things can be sensed if you pay close enough attention to them, my daughter," Grandmother said in a soft tone filled with wisdom.

"Mother, she has crossed the line this time! Bringing such shame to our family. Remember when that girl back home who ran away with her lover? We might as well be mentioned in the same category as her family now," Mother replied furiously. Clearly the night's rest had not eased her anger or changed her perspective.

"It is not the same thing! Zahra has not run away with anyone! She said she has not done anything to disrespect us, and I believe her. All she has done is got to know a potential suitor, what is wrong with that, I ask?" Grandmother said in my defence.

"With respect Mother, you are losing your mind. There's no room in our culture for love marriage! Running around with some stranger; letting them touch you and grab you and—*tobah tobah*—God knows what else she has done," Mother said with hint of disgust in her voice.

I buried my face further down into the depths of shame as I listened.

"Calm down my girl! I know my Zahra is as pure as snow! I will not have you or anyone say anything like that about my Zahra ever again. Do you hear me?" Grandmother protested firmly.

It felt so good to hear someone stand up for me like this. I don't think anyone ever had before. I was imagining Mother shaking her head at Grandmother's comment, "pure as snow."

Yeah right! I thought about what "It" did to me and I didn't feel pure at all. If only that hadn't happened. If only it was a figment of my imagination. Sometimes when I remembered some things "It" did to me, it was almost like my brain could not register that those things really did happen.

I started to second guess my own memory. It was almost like I was accusing myself of fabricating the whole thing. The mind may want to forget but the body remembers it all.

I had recently read in psychological journals at uni, that our brains are wired like this. It's as if our mind is protecting itself from those traumatic memories to help us cope or survive.

"Anyway, what is so wrong about marrying the person one loves?" Grandmother had continued speaking. "Is it a bad thing to really get to know the person before agreeing to sign your entire life over to them? Now where is the harm in that?" she said as if she'd had a sudden epiphany.

"Look at my poor girl Injilla and what she went through. She barely knew the man before she agreed to marry him," Grandmother said in disdain.

"Yes, Mother but look at the list of arranged marriages in our family alone that have worked compared to how many love marriages you can name that have lasted," I heard Mother say in reply.

"That is because love marriage couples were disowned, so we don't even know what happened with them. And in terms of marriages in our family, let's just say that some of us make do with what we have, but it doesn't necessarily mean we are happy," Grandmother said in reply.

"My girl, our children are born from us but are unfortunately not for us," I heard her continue, before a silence lingered after that.

I needed a moment to process this but I was having trouble getting my head around it. It really seemed like Grandmother was on my side. She was representing me out there and trying to convince Mother to change her mind.

"Mother there is no room for love marriage in our culture," my mother replied in total disagreement with Grandmother. "And if arranged marriages have worked for so many decades why change this now? We have lived experience that this works and that love marriages are great in the beginning but fizzle out."

"We definitely had lots of love marriages back home that worked really well, but it was at the expense of losing all family ties due to the dishonour that was connected with such practice," Grandmother responded in a frustrated tone. "It was taboo to talk about it let alone mention a couple who had married for love and who had succeeded in their relationship," she went on.

"I think, my girl, it is time to free us women and the men too, to choose who we want to spend the rest of our lives with," Grandmother stated firmly.

"People think it is easy for the men but hard on the women, but truth be told that is not the case. It is a forced decision on them both. So many men too have had to suffocate their hearts in order to uphold the honour of their family." Grandmother's voice was fading so I leaned against my bedroom door to hear her better.

The conversation seemed to have paused for the moment, so I finally got up from the back of the door and sat on my bed in disbelief that Grandmother was actually trying to stand up to Mother and help me and Humza be together! Not that I thought it would work with Mother, but I was really touched by Grandmother's kindness towards me.

But I wondered whether she would feel the same if she knew about me and "It." I felt my entire body ache as I got back in to bed, thankful that it was a Saturday, so I didn't have to worry about rushing to uni. But after all this I didn't think going to uni would even be on the table anymore.

As I lay there, I dreaded the thought of going back out to the living room and facing the queue of disappointed faces that would be staring at me. My body felt heavy, and my heart felt lonely. I needed to work on my assessment, which was due next week, but I was not able to concentrate while streaks of worry about Mother, Humza, and uni haunted me.

Chapter 37

When I finally left my bedroom that evening, after what felt like forever, Mother and Bahba were seated on the sofa along with Grandmother. Aunt Inji was there too, seated at the dining table. It seemed as if I had interrupted an important discussion by being there.

I went to greet and kiss Grandmother's hand. Then I said hello to Mother to which she turned her face in the opposite direction. *Exactly what I expected.* Bahba responded to my hello with what sounded like a mumble while Aunt Inji got up and hugged me tightly.

This is just what I need. The hug is giving me the strength to face what's waiting for me next. I can feel so much tension in the room.

I let go of Aunt Inji and sat next to her at the dining table. My face was flushed pink with worry and my eyes were puffy from all the crying.

"We were just talking …," Aunt Inji said, when Mother abruptly interrupted.

She stood up from the couch, unwillingly looked in my direction and said, "Who told you to come out here? This discussion doesn't need your input!"

"My girl you be quiet! She needs to be here as it involves her and her future," Grandmother quickly said in a slightly annoyed tone.

I could sense the tension in the room escalate even more between Mother and Grandmother.

And I know I am the cause of this.

"But Mother, this *faisha* has done enough to tarnish our family's name in the community..." Mother's voice was rising but Grandmother suddenly interrupted her tirade.

"Do not use that word ever again to refer to my Zahra! I will not stand for it. Learn to listen to your elders particularly your own mother, my girl," she snapped.

"What kind of example are you setting for Zahra and Injilla?" Grandmother continued as Mother stepped back and almost fell back into the couch with a puzzled look on her face.

"If you say horrible things like this about your own daughter then what hope does she have to survive in the community?"

"Learn to stand with your children and support them. Particularly as women we need to stand with each other in solidarity!" Her head and her chest were held out proudly.

This was the first time I had heard Grandmother get so fired up about anything! I could feel my throat tighten. As nice as it was to have someone from my family stand up in my defence, I couldn't help but feel uncomfortable. I looked up at everyone seated in the room, realising the pain I had caused them all, over my own happiness.

Without further thought I blurted out, "Grandmother please forgive me. Forgive me for causing you all so much pain and hurt. That is not at all what I want for you all.

"I want to make you all proud of me and I want only to contribute to your happiness instead of causing you all so much grief for my own selfishness!" I exclaimed sincerely.

"I want you all to know that my family comes above everything for me. Including above myself and my happiness. I will do what you want and marry whom you want me to marry, no questions asked!" I said convincingly. I just wanted them to be happy and I wanted this veil of pain and disappointment to be lifted.

How could I be so selfish! Blinded by Humza's love, I have forgotten all that my family have done for me and all the tribulations they have been through. I am here because of their hard work and because they took such a leap of faith by migrating to this foreign land. All so that we can all have a good life away from the pains of war.

"A bit too late for that Zahra!" Mother said softly under her breath before Grandmother interrupted.

"Child you have not done anything wrong or new for that matter. Love marriage happened a lot back home, it is just taboo to talk about it or acknowledge it in the community," Grandmother said in my defence.

"My child I am proud of you and the young lady you have become. Always thinking of others and putting their needs before yours. But this is a matter of a lifetime. My child, you need to make this decision with all your heart and mind," Grandmother said as she looked straight at me.

My heart was heavy again, but this time not with pain but with warmth. It was like the heat of the Sydney sun draping all over me as I lowered my gaze to avoid Grandmother seeing my eyes welling up with tears, which descended on both sides of my face. I tried hard to maintain my composure.

"We only want your happiness, my child," I heard Bahba say softly.

"And I know you my daughter—you would never do anything intentionally to disgrace yourself or your family," Bahba went on, to my surprise.

I knew Bahba was much more reasonable than Mother but I didn't expect him to come around so quickly!

Aunt Inji placed her hand in mine with a tissue in between and gently squeezed it as I looked up at her thankfully. It must have been her magic skill of persuasion that had worked on Bahba, reaping such fruit!

"You have our support. But as your elders we need to do our part and make sure Humza is the person he appears to be and we will conduct our own investigation in the community," Bahba said gravely.

"We trust your judgment, but we have lived experience to guide us. We don't want to go into things blindly like we did with Injilla and Omar," he said with a downhearted tone.

"I will also get your brother to ask around about Humza in his group of friends and see what he can surface. If he is taking drugs, is violent or has a criminal history or gambling—things like that," Bahba said supportively.

"I only want what is best for you, which includes

for you to be safe and happy my dear daughter," Bahba said emotionally.

"What is wrong with you all! You are so weak, enabling her to behave like this...," Mother lashed out angrily before Bahba abruptly interrupted her.

"Shut up for once woman!" Bahba said aggressively as he stood up on the spot.

Mother cowered into the couch. I had never heard Bahba get angry like this before, especially at Mother. I had always thought that Bahba feared Mother's anger and rage. But perhaps he was not scared but rather turned a blind eye to her behaviour out of love and respect that he has for her.

Bahba sat back down and Mother leaned back in her seat, remaining quiet. I could see out of the corner of my eye, Grandmother giving Mother the side eye, shaking her head in pure disapproval.

"My dear daughter in the meantime, while we do what we need to do, I want you to respect our one rule and stay away from Humza. I will not restrict you from your studies or treat you like a prisoner, but I ask you to keep your distance from him for the time being," Bahba said convincingly as he sent a cold glance in Mother's direction.

I gently nodded my head up and down as a sign of my acceptance and adherence to his request.

Which was not asking much. I must have still been in shock about this meeting and everyone's reaction. Except Mother's of course.

"And if anyone interferes with this plan, so help me god!" Bahba exclaimed as looked in the direction where Mother was seated. Bahba then stood up and came towards me and laid a gentle kiss on the top of my head. He stroked the side of my face with his hand to wipe away my tears.

"My girl, no more crying. No one has died. Go get cleaned up and focus on your studies," Bahba said encouragingly.

"Life will bring many challenges and this is just one small one," he added as he tapped me lovingly on the head before leaving the room.

I am in complete shock! This is not at all the outcome that I had expected. Whatever ends up happening after this, I am okay with it because I trust Bahba's judgment and know that I am well cared for.

Even Imran was supportive when he found out, sneaking into my room to let me know he was happy that I'd found a "nuttier" person than myself willing to marry me. He said that Afghan brothers treated their sisters like chattel and acted like their bodyguards; like pieces of meat that needed to be guarded from men. Wanting to chain their sisters or even in some cases denying having a sister at all! Imran clearly took after Bahba, a wise and true gentleman, that was for sure.

Aunt Inji stood up from next to me and hugged me and I broke down even more. I was so touched that my family cared so much for me and wanted my happiness. And that they were willing to step over any cultural hurdles for my happiness.

As I stood there in Aunt Inji's embrace I realised that there were lots of people who absolutely loved me and wanted me to be happy. Bahba, my brother, Grandmother, and Aunt Inji.

Even though I craved and pined for Mother's love, I needed to accept that this may never happen. I needed to make peace with this, because I knew Mother had a lens that she saw me through and she saw a sexually abused child. And the worst part was that she blamed me for what happened.

I didn't know for sure, but maybe the rest of the family would feel differently to Mother if they knew about "It." After all, if they could come around and accept my relationship with Humza, then maybe there was a chance they would see the abuse with "It" for what it actually was, child sexual abuse!

Chapter 38

As I sat on the metal bench near the library, I looked up at the sky. I could feel the warmth of the sun gently touching my skin every now and then, as the clouds continued to move around, occasionally sheltering me from its rays.

After so long I was finally feeling some peace. It was a nice feeling, it was liberating. In a perfect world I would have won Mother's love by now and would be feeling completely at peace, but I knew that no one lived in a perfect world. I was trying to appreciate what I had instead of longing for what I may never be able to attain.

"Thank goodness you're here! I have been going mad wondering what happened because you have not been coming to uni. I was thinking the worst!" Humza sat next to me with an anxious smile on his face.

I had totally forgotten that I have been away from uni for the past two days. I had been trying to put myself together to face Humza, forgetting what he might be going through without my presence.

I stood up and walked away.

"Hey Pretty Eyes, what's wrong? Where are you going?" he asked as he followed me along.

"My parents found out about us, that's why we can't be seen together," I said frantically looking around to see who is watching us.

"Oh no, how did they find out?" Humza asked with a confused expression on his face.

"It is a long story, but now is not the right time," I managed to say quickly as I kept walking.

"Hey, hey I know this is stressful, but we need to talk. Please don't shut me down," Humza said as he grabbed my wrist to bring me to a halt.

My mind was racing, and I didn't know how to make him understand that we have eyes on us here at uni.

"Meet me at the back of the uni, near B block, and I will explain everything. Just not here," I managed to quickly say before scurrying in the opposite direction.

As I stood waiting near B block, it wasn't long before Humza appeared, out of breath, with a thousand questions on his face, impatiently wanting to have answers.

"My Zahra, are you okay? We have been so careful.

How did they find out?" he asked inquisitively.

I love it when he calls me "my Zahra". It makes me feel desired, like I genuinely matter to him.

"I am okay. It has been a stressful few days let's just say that," I managed to say before I unleashed my anger at Soria.

"It was that Soria girl who is always hanging around us. She must have said something about us being together and it has now spread like wildfire in the community and reached Mother while she was at the butcher's shop," I exclaimed.

"Oh my god! We were so careful. I don't get it," Humza said confused as he rubbed his forehead trying to make sense of it all.

"Maybe we were so caught up in our bubble that we didn't see other people noticing us being together so much. They must have figured it out. Are we that obvious even though we were being so discrete?" he asked.

"Did your family come down hard on you? Please tell me, I am dying here!" Humza said desperately.

"Surprisingly, everyone took it well and Grandmother and Bahba have been super supportive. Mother of course is a different story," I managed to say.

"But we are not out of the woods, so to speak.

Bahba agreed to the relationship with one condition. For him to ask around about you in the community and if he gets positive feedback then is happy to support the relationship!" I said anxiously.

"Okay, that is good, but at the same time very worrying!" Humza said with a concerned look on his face.

"I am not very connected with the Afghan community; my parents are more active, but I do have some Afghan friends," he said.

"You don't have any skeletons in the closet do you Humza? Anything that we need to know about?" I asked, unsure what I expected his response to be but recognising it was coming from pure uneasiness.

"Nothing I haven't already told you. A few girlfriends in the past and I've been to a few night clubs back in the day. But I don't know if that's something your Bahba will see as condemning," he replied, slightly concerned that this may come back to haunt him.

I imagined that young people, particularly young men, had done many things that they looked back on and were not proud of. I hoped Bahba could relate to this and go easy on Humza.

"I am not into gambling or drinking or drugs. So that goes in my favour. I feel so under pressure right now," Humza said nervously.

"Okay let's say that Bahba doesn't approve of me then what?" he asked.

"I have said this to you before. I want you in my life one way or another. If not as my wife, then I need you in my life as my best friend. Because I can't imagine my life without you, now that I know what it can be like with you in it," Humza pleaded.

"I know Humza. This is hard on me too. Let's take it one step at a time and see how Bahba goes before we make any further decisions. But in the meantime, as hard as it is, we need to keep away from each other and respect Bahba's wishes. This will be a test for us both," I said knowing this would be really difficult for each of us.

Humza looked down at the ground as he kicked the tree branches with his shoes in frustration.

"Zahra, I am so worried. I will not be able to bear being away from you and can't imagine not having you in my life. This will break me!" he said as he came closer to me, gently touching each side of my shoulders with his hands. I saw in his eyes deep pain, fuelled by uncertainty.

His touch was gentle and soothing, yet it also brought an escalation in my heartbeat, sweaty palms, and difficulty swallowing. Humza had given me hope that life is not just filled with darkness. It had been exceedingly difficult for me to trust and let people into my life, or into my heart, but Humza felt right; he felt safe, he felt like home.

May God keep this light steady in my life and help pave the path to a bright future for us both.

Without thinking further or saying anything, I opened my arms and embraced Humza. We both needed this. Sometimes actions speak far louder than words ever can. With Humza in my arms, I could feel his heart beating fast against my chest as he stood still like a statue. I could sense he didn't expect this hug at all. Took Humza thirty seconds before he lifted his arms and embraced me.

"We are in this together, Humza. We need to remain positive and respect Bahba's wishes," I said as we stood there for a few minutes holding each other tight.

Chapter 39

One week and two days and there was still no news from Bahba about his investigation into Humza and his character in the community. I was getting increasingly anxious as the days passed. I couldn't help but feel my optimism dispersing into the air like a passing cloud up in the sky.

It had been very hard at home with Mother's glares and her backhanded comments. Sometimes I wished I had never met Humza, so I wouldn't have to be going through all this. At the same time, though, he is the best thing that has ever happened to me.

It was much the same at uni— I would bump into Humza around the classrooms and in the outdoor areas but knew I needed to keep my head down and ignore him. I could see it in his face that this was hard on him as well.

Grandmother always says, "There's no need to rush in life, what's meant for you will always arrive in its own time." I honestly believe this. I have faith in God and what he decides for me. If Humza and I are meant to be together, then no matter what, it will happen. But if we are not meant for each other, then something will come in the way and keep us apart.

I looked at the clock on my Nokia mobile phone that Bahba had got me a few days ago, saying that this was the latest model for this brand. It gave him peace of mind knowing I had this with me when I was out till late at uni and that I could call home any time if needed. Time seemed to be moving very slowly.

Usually, my days at uni were fast and busy but since I have been apart from Humza this has changed to a snail's pace. I pined to see him and speak with him. But when I did see him around uni grounds, I pretended that I didn't know him. If our eyes met by chance, he smiled at me, and I would get so self-conscious about who might be watching (and who might be reporting back to Mother and Bahba) that I would quickly look away.

My phone rang and I could see 'Bahba' on the screen. I answered the call, "*Salam* Bahba."

"*Walekum asalam* my daughter. I wanted to quickly let you know that I have asked around about Humza in the community and your brother has asked around about him as well," Bahba said.

My heart started to beat out of rhythm. Faster than it needed to, contemplating Bahba's decision.

"Everyone had nothing but good things to say about him and his family. I want you to find Humza and bring him home with you at once. I have made my decision. One which I think you will both be incredibly pleased with, my daughter," Bahba said as his voice took an emotional turn, but with a positive overtone.

"That is a relief Bahba. Okay I will find him and bring him with me. Thank you, Bahba," I managed to say as my heart filled with hope and excitement once again.

"Zahra, there was a song I would always sing for you when you were little, you may not remember it, but it went like this... 'My daughter is my daughter, better than 1000 sons. Even if the king comes with his entire army asking for her hand in marriage, I shall never give my daughter away,'..." Bahba sang as his voice shook with feeling.

My throat too tightened up, but I managed to say, "Oh Bahba, I will forever be your little girl! This will never change no matter what."

"I know my beautiful daughter Zahra. May Allah always guide and protect you. Bring Humza with you when you find him. We are all waiting for you both at the house. We need to talk about setting a wedding date!" Bahba said before saying goodbye and ending the call.

I was on cloud nine! My happy ending was becoming a reality, who would have thought this could happen? Definitely, not me! As my mind raced, I quickly grabbed my bag and headed off to find Humza as quickly as I could to share this amazing news with him.

I have never envisioned happiness for myself like this after what happened to me with "It." I had always felt that I was not worthy. Like I was dirty and that it was all my fault. Humza had given me hope and taught me to know my worth. Finally, I believed that I too deserved to have good things in my life.

* * *

I went to our usual sitting area, but he was nowhere to be seen. *Perhaps he has gone to the cafeteria?* I thought and quickly headed that way. There was no sign of him there either.

Where could he be? I wondered. The only place I could think of was the library. I continued to race towards the library, my heart bursting with excitement to share this good news with him.

As I frantically searched in the study area, I

finally found him in one of the private study rooms sitting with his books spread all around him.

I knocked on the door, two gentle taps before entering the room. Humza looked up from his books. An expression of both shock and excitement filled his face as he saw me. He stood up and came towards the door.

"Is everything okay? I thought you said we can't see each other," he asked in a concerned tone as he gently touched both sides of my arms with his hands.

"No, I am not okay! I just spoke with Bahba. Get ready to put up with me for the rest of your life!" I managed to say before bursting into tears as I wrapped my arms around him.

"Are you serious? This is great news!" Humza said as he hugged me, lifting me up off the floor, caught up with the excitement of the moment.

After a few seconds, he put me down, letting go from his embrace. He took a step back, his eyes teary and said, "This has been the most difficult time of my life! Not being able to speak with you and wondering whether I would lose you forever was driving me mad. Thank Allah for this news!" he said as he grabbed me again hugging me tighter this time.

"Hey, hey. Slow down. Bahba has asked us both to come to the house right now, everyone is waiting for us," I managed to say as I gently pulled away from him.

"What? Right now? This sounds so nerve wracking, but I am ready for anything if it means I can have you in my life, Pretty Eyes," he said with a smile on his face.

"Okay Mister Romeo let's get going before Bahba changes his mind," I said as I chuckled excitedly.

Humza frantically packed his books and pencil case. We hurried out of the library and towards the uni gates making our way to my house.

Is this really happening? I, Zahra, am getting showered with happiness. This feels so strange, so unreal, so foreign. But it feels so good!

As we exited the university gates, I couldn't help but look up to the skies above as if in a silent prayer. A secret conversation between me and the clouds. Or what lies beyond the clouds. *Thank you, God,* I silently whispered.

Anyone who has been impacted by the content of this novel can reach out to 1800 Respect for confidential support and information if they reside in Australia. If you are located overseas, please contact your local services for support.

For confidential practical crisis support, information and accommodation to escape domestic violence please reach out to your relevant state based crisis support service available 24/7:

Australian Capital Territory
Domestic Violence Crisis Service
02 6280 0900

New South Wales
NSW Domestic Violence Line
1800 656 463

South Australia
SA Domestic Violence Crisis Line
1800 800 098

Victoria
Safe Steps
1800 015 188

Queensland
DV Connect Women's Line
1800 811 811

DV Connect Mensline
1800 600 636

Western Australia
Women's Domestic Violence Helpline
1800 007 339

Men's Domestic Violence Helpline
1800 000 599

Tasmania
Safe at Home Family Violence Response and Referral Line
1800 633 937

Northern Territory
Dawn House Women's Shelter (Darwin)
08 8945 1388

Northern Territory (continued)

DAIWS: Crisis Accommodation– Single women (Darwin)
08 8928 1206

Katherine Women's Crisis Centre
08 8972 1332

DAIWS: Crisis Accommodation – Women & Children
08 8945 2284

If English is not your first language and would like the assistance of an interpreter first call the Translating and Interpreting Service (TIS) on 13 14 50. They can connect you with the service of your choice and interpret for you.

If you have trouble hearing or speaking you can contact the above services through the National Relay Service (NRS) in two easy steps:

1. Contact the NRS.
The main number to contact the National Relay Service (NRS) is 1300 555 727 for Voice Relay, or 1800 555 660 for the NRS Help Desk. You can also use other channels like TTY (133 677) or the NRS website (www.relayservice.com.au) to connect. The appropriate number depends on the specific service you need.

2. Give the number you wish to connect with.

Glossary

Afghan Word	English Meaning
Bahba	father, grandfather or respectful term for a wise old man
Dari	Afghani language
faisha	whore or slut
haram	any act that is forbidden by Allah
jhan	means 'soul' or 'life'; also used as a diminutive suffix attached to names and expressing intimacy, like an equivalent to 'darling' or 'dear'
khasgaree	when a young woman is visited by a suitor and his family with a proposal of marriage; her family are also present to decide on the suitability of the proposal
margh	death to you
Mullah	title used for Muslim clergy and mosque leaders
Salaams / Salam	means 'peace' and used to greet fellow Muslims
sofra	a cloth or low table for serving food
tobah tobah	an expression of disgust requiring the need to ask for forgiveness from Allah
toshak	a floor cushion or narrow mattress commonly used floor seating
Wah, wah	an expression like 'wow'
Walekum asalam	means 'peace' be upon you too and used in reply to when a Muslim greets another fellow Muslim

About the Author

Arzoo Faiz was born in Kabul Afghanistan and relocated to Pakistan before migrating to Australia when she was a child. She earned her Bachelor of Laws degree from University of Western Sydney, completed her postgraduate studies in law and was admitted as a lawyer in 2008. She has also attained a Bachelor of Social Sciences degree from Swinburne University of Technology.

Arzoo practised as a family law solicitor in private practice in Sydney for a short time before entering the field of domestic, family and sexual violence, where she currently works.

Arzoo is a proud mother of two amazing children and lives in the Hills area in Sydney with her husband and extended family.

She has harboured a passion for writing for as long as she can remember and has finally released her first novel in 2025: *The Skies Above: A Story of Hope.* This novel brings her two passions together, love of writing, and her desire to create much needed awareness about domestic, family and sexual violence, particularly in the culturally and linguistically diverse communities.

www.ingramcontent.com/pod-product-compliance
Lightning Source LLC
Chambersburg PA
CBHW011222190726
48287CB00008B/2707

* 9 7 8 1 7 6 4 2 7 3 1 0 7 *